※

VICE-CONSUL
PANAMA

In Harm's Way

RANDOLF HARROLD

 FriesenPress

Suite 300 - 990 Fort St
Victoria, BC, V8V 3K2
Canada

www.friesenpress.com

ISBN
978-1-4602-8717-0 (Hardcover)
978-1-4602-8718-7 (Paperback)
978-1-4602-8719-4 (eBook)

1. FICTION, MYSTERY & DETECTIVE

Distributed to the trade by The Ingram Book Company

DEDICATION

To Canadian diplomats, whose exploits are legend in pursuit of fairness and justice in the sometimes no-man's land of diplomatic service. And to Diane, the mother of our children, my true love, artist, and frequent partner in exploring the adventures life has on offer.

This is a work of fiction. Any representations of historical events, persons historical, living, or dead, or references to real locales, have been used fictitiously.

PART ONE

October 1972

CHAPTER 1

The steamy air hit Rob Kingman in the face like a wall as the smiling Latina swung open the heavy cabin door. Ducking through, he unfolded his tall form and reached for the handrail. He climbed gingerly down the stairs of the twin turboprop, briefcase in hand, glancing upward at the lush green palms surrounding the airport terminal, distorted as they were through the shimmering vapors rising off the hot tarmac. Rob smiled.

It had been a short flight from San Jose to Panama City. The macho pilots had hot-dogged the landing with a steep approach and had taxied swiftly up to the gate, the tight turns on descent reminiscent of how the Red Baron would have landed his World War One biplane. As a pilot, he admired their cowboy style, but as a husband, he was glad Sophie wasn't along. Steep turns and erratic movement were definitely not her forte. Even at country fairs, she studiously avoided Ferris wheels and roller coasters.

He pushed open the glass door and was met with a rush of somewhat cooler air. At least the terminal had air-conditioning. Brandishing his diplomatic passport, Rob approached the scowling, moon-faced officer seated on a stool behind a wood podium.

"La primera visita, señor?"

"Sí, yo soy el vicecónsul canadiense, acreditado en Panamá, residente en San José de Costa Rica."

"Bienvenido! Su Español no es tan malo!"

The man's scowl transformed into a grin as his entry stamp hand came down with a thump.

"Pasar bien! Enjoy!"

Rob passed through the special laneway for VIPs, and then, with a nod from the immigration police who had been watching his progress, he was through. As he bent to collect his one small bag, he glanced up at the throng of competing helpers shouting at him and one another, touting their services. Careful to avoid pickpockets, he pushed through the tangle of faces and hands, smiling grimly and repeating *"No! Gracias,"* every few steps.

With relief, he pushed through the doors at the front of the terminal to the line of decaying yellow taxis. A middle-aged black man, likely Trinidadian or Jamaican, hurried towards him from his taxi, parked somewhat apart from the others. With a smile he took Rob's case and conducted him to his car. He bowed slightly and opened the rear door with his right hand extended, then passed behind and put Rob's bag in the trunk with his left. A moment later, he slid into the driver's seat.

"Take me to the Hotel Panama, please, *señor* ; I'm late for an appointment," Kingman ordered somewhat breathlessly in Spanish, as he settled into the back seat, which puffed mould and the smell of sweat through cracks in the ancient leatherette.

"Johnny at yo' service. In a hurry suh? I be go'an Paseo Colon, pas' de *Ministerio de Seguridad Pública,* d' mos' direct route t'ru hell!" nodded the black *taxista* in a lilting

Caribbean twang. Rob could see his wry smile in the mirror, which reflected the widely spaced, severely blood-shot whites, or rather yellows, of his eyes, which crinkled at the sides.

"Yes, I'm late for a meeting. Is the Ministry as bad as all that? I'll be visiting there tomorrow."

"Well, f' foreigners it's not so bad, I s'pose, but for us Panamanians, we haf' t' keep our noses clean, and some-times it's hard t' tell wha' it means. You look like some kind of official, so I 'magine your comin' an' goin' won't be troublesome! Where you come from?"

Glancing over his left shoulder, he swung out, horn blaring as the battered yellow taxi shuddered and lurched into the traffic. The acrid smell of exhaust and burning oil now filtered up through the floorboards and mixed with the humid, choking air.

"Yeah, I hope so. I'm the new Canadian vice-consul based in Costa Rica, down here to check up on a school-teacher who's missing. Since it's my first visit, maybe you could show me around later. Hit the high spots so I get the lay of the land, so to speak."

"You bet. I be dere. At yo' service, sir!"

Sitting back he recalled, wiping his neck with a hand-kerchief, that dealing with the welfare of Canadians abroad was what they had said in his briefings in Ottawa he would be doing. But he felt considerable anxiety about finding the missing missionary in a foreign country he was visiting for the first time. His Ambassador in San Jose had told him to line up a few meetings through the British Consul who was so far handling the case, and rely on his experienced advice.

The landscape flashed by quickly for a preoccupied Rob. Two storey whitewashed buildings with red roof tiles alternated with similar buildings with rusted corrugated iron roofs. The air seemed palpable with the smell of mould permeating everywhere. They passed Balboa's statue and Rob gazed out over the Pacific as the Conquistador had for the first time in 1513. He fingered his yellow fever vaccination certificate for reassurance, as they passed a sign for Miraflores Locks, the most famous of the Panama Canal pumping stations, recalling how the French engineer DeLessups had been defeated by the disease in the late 1800's. Finally, Johnny braked hard and swerved rather violently, knocking Rob's head against the window, as they turned into the magnificent driveway of the white Hotel Panama, framed with royal palms, pink magnolias and lush bougainvillea- and came to a gasping stop at the door.

Johnny grinned triumphantly, "We' here, Sir!"

Reception directed him. After bounding up four flights of stairs, suitcase in hand, Rob arrived out of breath for his meeting with the Christian Missionary Service Committee in a fourth floor room, not pausing before pushing open the door. The dour Mennonite elders, far from their Manitoba roots, turned startled, sunburned faces towards a sweaty, disheveled Rob. To a man, their faces expressed distain at the young vice-consul who, in his inexperience, had not paused to compose himself and knock.

Nevertheless, they politely rose all together, and one by one extended their gnarled hands to be shaken before returning to their seats around the dark, tropical wood table.

"Rob Kingman, Canadian Vice-Consul."

"Milton Eisenhauer," said a stout man with slick silver hair.

"Not the president?" Rob smiled, trying to lighten the atmosphere.

"No. That was my uncle, Dwight," Milton said, stone faced. "But he died some time ago." Full stop. No smile. No elaboration.

"Any news?" demanded their apparent leader, Clayton Kratz, who pushed his square wire-framed glasses up his pointed nose with his index finger as he sat down. Henry Friesen and Rudy Wiebe nodded impatiently. While they were happy to see a real Canadian presence in Panama, finally, it had been four days since the reported disappearance of the young missionary teacher, and they were very anxious for progress.

They were not at all impressed with Rob's hurried arrival, and they wasted no time in commenting on the apparent lack of resources in the field. The first report of trouble had come to him through the British consulate, as was normal practice where there was no resident Canadian representation.

"Well, nothing new, yet," said Rob. "I haven't had the opportunity to meet with the British Embassy for a briefing. I thought perhaps you could tell me what you know so far."

"Don't think you'll get much joy from Middleton," growled Wiebe, black greasy curls framing a round florid face. "We haven't, anyways."

Henry Friesen ventured, "I teach with Kevin Voth at our school for refugees. Nice guy and family man. One of us, you know, *heh, heh.* Of late, he'd been giving some extra English classes to a student who's been struggling. Told him it wasn't expected and could even be dangerous in the *barrio,* but he was quite dedicated and wanted to go the extra mile. It was after one of these sessions four days ago that he disappeared. So far, Middleton and the Panamanian authorities have given us all help short of actual assistance in finding him. Hope you can do better."

Rob smiled anxiously and said he hoped so, too. Before flying out of San Jose, Rob had called Jack Middleton, the British consul. Middleton had not been able to give him any new info. He'd said he would have an update from *Seguridad Pública* by the time Rob arrived, so Kingman was anxious to leave the meeting and get down to his room. He found his cabana located beside the pool, positioned in a virtual forest of tropical greenery.

As he approached his room, he batted aside branches that had encroached on the gravel path. He blinked. The advice of the minister's assistant, Tony, resurfaced. "Since you are new to all this, a little advice is in order. There are at least two angles you have to watch for: the first is that this group of missionaries are from the minister's constituency and will be expecting special service, so they will watch you like hawks and complain constantly. Second: the head of security you'll have to work with is a close confident of President Torrijos, who is angling to politically embarrass the Americans over the lack of Panamanian sovereignty over the Canal Zone. So watch out for something. Don't know what it will be."

It was later and the evening was darkening when Jack Middleton appeared in front of the open-air bar on the opposite side of the enormous pool. He had come from the British Embassy down the block and mopped profuse sweat from his neck with a thoroughly dank handkerchief. Jack was of late middle age, and was clad in a heavy grey, three-piece striped wool suit, totally inappropriate for the tropical climate. It rumpled over his dumpy, overweight body. Thinning gray-brown hair in need of a London barber fell over his craggy eyebrows. Rivulets of perspiration ran down his temples to disappear under his collar. A well-worn pipe was firmly clenched in his stained teeth. He and Rob shook hands.

"Glad you could make it down to Panama so quickly," he loosened his tie, as they sat to await their badly needed drinks. "This started out as a straight case of a missing person, but has gotten rather lumpy, I should say." Rob strained to catch his broad accent.

"What do you mean, 'lumpy?' Do you mean political? Our Minister seems to be taking a close interest in the case. I met with the missionary committee this afternoon, and it wasn't very pleasant. But there could be more than that. Tell me."

"Well, every chance they get, *Los panameños* stick it to the Americans. Subtly of course, and with a smile," wheezed Middleton, with a sallow smile, except where the florid patches burst through. "But behind the Americans' backs, it's all about shedding the colonial legacy and gaining sovereignty over the Canal. You'll get inkling, I'm sure, when you meet the head of security, Manuel Antonio Noriega, *El jefe!* I was a bit delayed because I was waiting for a call back about an appointment for you, which, by the way, is tomorrow morning at nine. Noriega's in charge of pretty well everything around here and runs this tiny country like a personal fiefdom."

"Then the president's just a figurehead?" Rob prodded.

"Well, no. Of course, he does it all on behalf of President Torrijos," Middleton said. "Noriega does all the dirty work, behind the scenes: like keeping the opposition in check, or anyone else who might have the temerity to complain about the corruption and graft."

"Well, how does that relate to our missing Canadian?"

"Kevin Voth has been missing for four days. It's inconceivable that, with an ear in practically every household, *El jefe* doesn't know where he is. Something's cooking on the back burner. He's also made clear that he's not keen on dealing with Britain, who they still regard as a colonial power, when it's a Canadian matter. It may also have something more to do with the fact that Canada now sits on the UN Security Council."

After their third drink in the bar, they ordered what turned out to be a long dinner of rice and beans, ripe plantains, and steak, which lasted well into the evening. Over coffee, an entertaining Middleton shared a seemingly endless repertoire of war stories about his challenging consular adventures, from Cairo to Kinshasa, Colombo to Rabat.

It was nearly midnight when Rob wished him good night at the front door of the hotel, where a fatigue-clad soldier stood guard. As he returned to his cabana on the other side of the pool, he undressed and pulled on his swimming trunks. Out on the path again, his flip-flops scrunched in the gravel, as he walked the few yards to a lonely cane chair beside the pool, and shed his towel.

The night was quiet except for an occasional passing car outside the whitewashed wall between him and the street. He plunged into the deserted pool, swam a few lengths, and returned to his cabana.

Refreshed, he let the day's events flow through his mind. As a chorus of cicadas and tree frogs came through the open venetian blind, Rob got up, naked, to peer out through the window slats into the tropical foliage and the steamy black night. Despite the lack of breeze, the leaves rustled beside his cabana. He slipped on the white terry-cloth hotel robe, turned off the light, and opened the door.

He took a few tentative steps down the walkway over-hung by palms and bougainvillea. Not a breath of air stirred over the sultry pool. He peered into the dark and saw no one. Despite the heat, he shivered ever so slightly and turned back to the cabana. Once inside, he switched on the air conditioner to shut out the night noise. Sleep came fitfully.

An explosion and a bright blue flash startled Kingman bolt upright in his bed. Acrid, choking smoke coming from burning wires and plastic stung his nostrils and burned his eyes. He clambered in the dark for the phone to call the desk.

The night clerk responded almost immediately, as if waiting outside. He was accompanied by a *Seguridad Pública* officer, dressed in sloppy fatigues and carrying a stub-nosed machine gun, cigarette hanging between his lips. He examined the smoking air conditioner and then stood back, shaking his head but not saying a word.

Hotel management was profuse in its apologies for what they said was a faulty air conditioner. Kingman was moved in the middle of the night to a luxurious, air-conditioned suite on a higher floor of the hotel tower.

Just as his pre-dawn fitful slumber returned, his wake-up call startled him out of solid sleep.

CHAPTER 2

As the taxi ground to a halt in front of *Seguridad Pública*, ahead of his meeting with Manuel Antonio Noriega, Rob glanced up through his open car window at the imposing four-story sandstone villa and brushed some sweat from his throbbing temple. The building reminded him of a film he had seen of Mussolini in wartime Rome. The short, shadowy despot had addressed a chanting crowd from a balcony of a building much like this one on the Piazza Venezia.

Rob's apprehension grew as he was escorted down a darkened hall on the fourth floor by two stern-faced, fatigue-clad young officers with snub-nosed submachine guns cradled against their chests. They came to a halt in front of two tall mahogany doors. A brief rap, and, *"Sí, entra,"* came imperiously from within.

The door was opened and Rob strode unaccompanied across a wide expanse of Persian rug, towards a short figure who was rising from behind an enormous desk, framed in the light of French windows leading out to the balcony.

Hand extended, gravelly voice booming, Manuel Antonio Noriega came around. *"Señor* Kingman, welcome to Panama! I understand your first night was somewhat disturbed."

Noriega grasped Rob's hand and shook it firmly, his left hand coming to rest on Kingman's shoulder, and his piercing brown eyes peered up into the Canadian's face. His broad nose and fleshy face, pockmarked by childhood smallpox, gave him the appearance of a boxer. Three stars on the epaulets of his crisp, khaki uniform marked his rank as that of a lieutenant colonel.

"The hotel staff reported some malfunction of an air conditioner or something. You weren't hurt were you?"

Taken aback by this brusque, well-informed but friendly greeting, Rob marveled at how the word of such an apparently minor incident had come to the head of security so rapidly. It was somewhat off-putting. Rob flashed back to the British consul's cautions the evening before.

"No, I wasn't hurt, but it was quite an introduction to Panama. Your organization seems to be very efficient and well informed!"

Noriega laughed, slightly mocking, "No, no! Well, you know; we have to take care of our VIPs! We get reports about our important guests from hotels and other places around town. We need to be sure you are... well looked after."

Dismissing any further discussion, he continued, "Before we get down to the business at hand, I want to show you something."

Noriega wheeled and strode to the French windows, nodding for Kingman to follow him into the sunlight on the small balcony. There was no chanting crowd on the paved compound below, just a large number of bright blue cars.

"How do you like my new fleet of Dodge Darts? They'll allow my agents to get around more effectively to conduct investigations, like that for your missing school teacher!" beamed Noriega. "US aid is very generous, you know."

Kingman nodded his head and smiled in affirmation while marking the incongruity of the white roundels stencilled on the doors, boldly proclaiming "*Policía Secreta*"!

"Congratulations," he mumbled lamely.

They returned to comfortable chairs, where *café con leche* and rolls waited on side tables.

"I want to assure you of our fullest support and cooperation in the ongoing investigation of Kevin Voth's disappearance," offered Noriega. "I understand he was doing very good work teaching English to a group of new refugees."

" Oh, really? The Mennonite Service Committee hadn't mentioned this? Is there more?"

" Well he's gone missing while teaching someone extra lessons in the barrio," went on Noriega, "which is strange for someone who apparently spoke good Spanish, and was seemingly a well-liked fellow. Knew how to get around."

"Seems as if you have been taking a close interest in the case," mused Rob.

"You could say that," Noriega said stiffly. " His wife is quite distressed, I understand, though she took two days to tell us he disappeared, according to my investigating officer."

"You have no clues as to where he might be?" Rob's incredulity showed. Middleton had observed that through his network of watchers, Noriega knew everything. Rob hoped he wasn't hiding something.

"My men are doing their best, and they report frequently to me directly on this one, involving a foreigner," Noriega chastened, "though we have no progress to report at the moment. With the late start, we're still in the fact-finding stage, interviewing those people who apparently saw him last, and trying to determine just what happened after he left them. Of course, we've heard from Middleton, the British consul, on your behalf, as well as that overbearing Service Committee."

Kingman noted the Miami twang in Noriega's excellent English, and the disdain in his voice. He had heard that he trained with the CIA.

"Thank you," Rob said. "I'll have to get on with some calls myself. Seeing his wife is a priority, and perhaps visiting the school where he taught."

"Sure, go ahead. My investigating officer will take you to help things along. I've got our top man, Captain Rios, on the job. And I'll send you updates to the Hotel Panama as our investigation progresses, if that's where you are setting up headquarters."

Rob declined Noriega's offer of accompaniment, despite his insistence, though it would be more difficult, his not knowing Panama City. He preferred to be less directed in his own investigation.

"I have some other items to follow up not concerning the investigation, so thank you," Rob was firm.

"Well I wish you luck. Stay out of trouble," Noriega said menacingly. He was not pleased.

Johnny was waiting for Rob as he exited the building. "Back to the Hotel Panama, please," he frowned.

"How you like it, boss?" Johnny watched him furtively in the rear view mirror, as he skillfully negotiated the heavy traffic. " T'ings goin' well?"

"OK, I guess. Noriega seems a very insistent sort of guy

and doesn't take it well when you refuse his help."

"You could say dat. Seems he got a reputation for not takin' no for an answer!"

"Yes. Can you take me on a tour after lunch? I need to find my way around without extra help from *Seguridad*, you follow?"

"You bet. I be waitin' boss."

After lunch and a short siesta, they began with the obligatory stop at the Balboa statue overlooking the Pacific. The tour progressed past the alternating riches and squalor that made up Panama City. Cinderblock low-rises, older adobe houses, and rusting tin shanties alternating with handsome walled white villas set in the palms.

The heat and humidity were elevated and Johnny droned on, throwing comments over the seat. Just as Kingman was leaning back to close his eyes, there was a rap on the window. The taxi had come to a stop at the checkpoint entrance to the Miraflores Lock.

A handsome young American MP with short-cropped blond hair leaned towards the open window and demanded, "May I see your passport, sir?" Kingman struggled to right himself. For a moment, he hurriedly patted his pockets, and then realized it was in his suit jacket, which he had taken off in the heat and folded on the seat beside him.

"Cunadjun diplomat, eh, Sir? Welcome to the Zone. I'm from Deetroit, so I know your country well. Could use a little of that ice and snow at the moment!" he grinned, deep sunburn and red peeling nose. He passed back the document, touching his forehead with a casual salute.

As the taxista gunned his shuddering steed down the

newly paved highway, Kingman marvelled at the contrast of the Zone's well-tended flower beds, clean roadways, and brightly painted buildings.

The massive Miraflores locks spread before them, a miracle of French and American engineering at the time they were completed in 1913.

Out of the taxi and standing at the edge of a barrier across the lock, Rob stretched, now fully awake with a rush of wonder and anxiety. He touched his forehead and shielded his eyes from the full sun. In his amazement, he watched as an enormous bulk carrier rose fifty-four feet as the chamber flooded, and a container ship, heading in the opposite direction, dropped the fifty-four feet as water flooded into the twin locks over the course of a few minutes. Then, the two ships went on their way, one transiting westward to Balboa on the Pacific, passing under the great Bridge of the Americas. The other sailed easterly, towards Lake Gatun and the Atlantic.

He stood pondering, recalling the ministerial assistant's admonition to watch for *it* coming. Watch for what? How could the disappearance of a Canadian school teacher be linked to the dispute over the American ownership of the Canal?

In the briefing center Kingman had poured over histories and papers on issues in Panama in preparation for his assignment. Now having seen it, Kingman understood the massive undertaking in work, capital, and lives that the Canal represented. He understood the tumultuous history of the construction of the Panama Canal, the struggle for independence, and the signature of a flawed 1903 treaty that would have granted the United States a renewable lease in perpetuity of the land that held the Canal. But, it had been misinterpreted as a "ninety-nine year lease" due to misleading wording included in an Article of the agreement that apparently did not confer the right for the US to renew the lease indefinitely.

So here was some leverage, he thought as looked into the distance towards the Atlantic, for the Panamanian claim of sovereignty.

And there was further contention, in that the chief engineer of the French canal company had not been authorized to sign treaties on behalf of Panama without Panamanian review. It was this treaty that had become a disputed diplomatic issue between the two countries, especially following the Second World War, when the Canal Zone became a strategic base for more than eighty thousand troops in the defense of North and South America should the Cold War heat up.

It was also a key economic base that distributed through the Canal Zone a large share of goods and materiel for the whole region. Panama was now pressing for a UN Security Council meeting to review the situation, which could become a threat to peace and stability in South America.

Kingman frowned and touched his forehead, trying to piece together what he knew with what he was experiencing. Meanwhile the taxista continued to chatter on, explaining the functioning of the canal to him. But Rob just puzzled over how the disappearance of Kevin Voth could possibly be connected to the politics of the Canal?

He was ready to discount it, when Johnny cut through his thoughts with, "You look like you're losin' concentration, if I may say so. Wanna go for a cruise along the canal side, just to get a little fresher air out in t' country?"

They stood gazing along the side of the canal where the proposed drive would take place. Johnny gestured and pointed to a lower lush bushy area. "Looks strange," he exclaimed, "d' yu see those vultures circling just above the bananas and canebrake? Let's go down there, jus' t' see."

"See what?" queried Rob. He did not share Johnny's enthusiasm to go down and see. As the taxi bumped off the asphalt road onto the gravel track that led towards the low-lying area, apprehension rose in Kingman's chest. Why was he taking him here?

They pulled up off the road. The driver nodded, raising his chin, "It's too sof'. We best get out an' walk from here."

Disgusting black vultures rose with squawks and flaps in the steamy air behind the thick canebrake as they approached. Kingman could see a slight parting in the mass of tangled greenery where something had passed.

"S' very odd," the driver grunted, exhaling as he bent to remove his shoes – he wasn't wearing socks – and fold up his pant cuffs.

Not convinced, Rob stood his ground. "You go ahead and check it out, Johnny. I'll wait here."

"OK, sure. I be back fo' you if it looks exciting!" He turned and moved cautiously towards the opening.

"Got to watch for snakes an' nasty critters of all kinds!" shouted Johnny nervously over his shoulder, voice rising. He was really getting into it now. The greenery moved and bent where Johnny pushed through and for a few moments Rob could hear only splashing and grunting. Then silence. In a few moments he was back, dirty green mud almost to his knees, eyes bulging, his face a lighter shade of gray.

"Like I tol' yuh," he whistled through clenched teeth, "very strange. You'll want to see this!"

They struggled through an opening in the cane for a few paces before they came upon a small clearing. Grass was pressed into the mud, where a partially clad man lay face down in the shallow water. He was naked to the waist. Obviously very dead. Stab wounds lined his back on either side of his spine, and blood seeped between his shoulder blades. Flies swarmed around the wounds, enlarged where the vultures had been picking at them. Shocked, the two men looked at each other sombrely.

Johnny moved first, and bent as if to lift him up by an arm to get a look at his face.

"Don't touch him!" Kingman shouted. "We have to leave the crime scene just as it is for the investigators. We don't want to go on messing it up."

On the way back to the Miraflores checkpoint, Kingman pondered what he was going to say to the MPs. There was a good chance this could be Voth. He was uncertain though, because so far he was just missing-no indication there had been foul play in his disappearance. Still, how many thirty year old Caucasians were likely to have come to grief in such a small place at that exact same time? And odd that Johnny had been so insistent to have a look.

The Americans asked Kingman and the driver to accompany them back to the scene. A five man investigation team slogged through the mud in green rubber boots. A beefy Southerner at the end of the line, hauled out a camera, stepped forward and bent and shot, and stepped back and shot.

"How'd you find him in here?" demanded the MP

Captain, suspiciously eyeing Johnny.

"Saw the vultures rising over the canebrake," put in Rob, "so Johnny thought we should investigate. I'm here in Panama looking for a missing Canadian. Seems strange that we might have actually stumbled on him here. But we'll need to have him identified."

Nodding and turning, the Captain said to the others, "The track through the cane and most of the scene has been pretty well messed up. So we may as well move the body to the morgue for identification and further investigation." He motioned to the paramedics now standing by to put the body into a bag and onto their stretcher.

"Take him back to the base hospital. We'll need to order an autopsy and get the coroner down for further investigation." Turning to Rob, he said, "Do you recognize him at all? Is he the guy you are looking for?"

"Can't really say for sure. I haven't seen a good picture of him yet," though it was battered and obscured by mud, Rob thought to himself the face looked a lot like the photo on the passport page that had been faxed from headquarters in Ottawa. " I'll fax you what ID information I have if you give me a number."

"OK, then we'll let you know the results wherever you are staying. Have to let Panamanian security know, too. Don't leave town until the situation is clear, Sir. And we want to interview the taxi driver. Right now. "

"Right. I'll be available at the Hotel Panama. I won't be going anywhere for a few days, or until after my missing Canadian does show up."

When Johnny returned Kingman to the Hotel Panama at dinnertime, there was a message waiting for him to call Noriega at a special number. "We're making some progress," boomed the gravelly voice at the other end. "We've found Voth's car in a *barrio* near the school where he teaches. It's where a lot of the refugees live. The funny thing is, there seems to be no sign of forced entry. It looks like he left it locked up, with his wedding ring and wallet in the glove compartment. Come down tomorrow morning and I'll give you a full debriefing. We may know more by then."

Rob held back on the discovery of a body in the Zone. He was quite sure it was Voth, but he wanted to give the Americans time to identify him. And he was unsure if he should raise the issue with Noriega just yet, or wait until the situation became somewhat clearer.

CHAPTER 3

Rob strode forward, hand held out to be shaken, but Noriega was fuming and ignored it. Eyes narrowing, he spat out angrily, "You didn't tell me when we spoke last night, Mr. Kingman, that you had discovered the body in the Canal Zone! I had to hear it from the American MPs. Some cooperation and sharing of information. I told you all I knew last night. What game are you playing? This is clearly a criminal investigation, and we don't want Americans treading all over a sovereign Panamanian affair."

"All I can say is I'm sorry. It slipped my mind when you called with news. It could have been an American from the Zone for all I knew," said Kingman unconvincingly. "I do apologize. Have the canal authorities identified the body?"

"Slipped your mind?" all diplomatic friendliness had left his voice. "You bet they have identified him, through a call to *us*." Manuel Noriega paused for dramatic emphasis, his dark eyes locking with Kingman's. "It's Kevin Voth. Appears he died somewhere else. Dumped in the Zone. Interesting to know how whoever took him there got past the checkpoint. May even be an American, eh?"

He plunged on, "this could be really complicated if we don't get full cooperation from the Americans. But so far, they've agreed to turn the body over this afternoon, I assume because he isn't an American citizen. They'll continue with their own investigation in any case, probably to prepare a cover-up."

Kingman was surprised at Noriega's speculations. As the unpleasant interview ended, he had resolved not to be cowed by Noriega's tirade, especially in light of the expansive accusations that were flying.

Both men agreed that Rob would accompany an investigating officer to Miriam Voth's home, where he would break the news. The officer would ask Mrs. Voth to accompany them to the morgue to make an identification. As he made his way back to the hotel, Kingman's apprehension over the whole situation grew, and he called his ambassador in Costa Rica to get his advice.

"Boy, it sure sounds messy," Craig Langman quipped. The ambassador was an old hand in Latin America, having served in Lima, Bogotá, and Buenos Aires, and was adept at handling such complications. He had been one of the Air Force officers demobilized and retrained after the war and his demeanour reflected his background. He was now a bit overweight and a heavy drinker and smoker, though this did not seem to bear on his effectiveness. And he was kind.

"You'll need to be very comforting with Miriam Voth. I'm sure she'll be very shocked that he's been murdered. She has young children too, doesn't she?"

Answering his own question, he went on, "Of course, there are the children to consider. I wouldn't provide any details yet about how he was found, especially about the wedding ring in the glove compartment. They may be important details in tracking down who is responsible for the killing. They also could be devastating to Miriam should it prove Kevin was meeting a secret lover or some such messy thing."

"That's what Noriega would like us to think at this stage," Rob interjected. "He was even throwing around accusations of a love triangle involving a jealous American who murdered Voth. That's how the body got into the Zone. Maybe setting up complicated sovereignty issues?"

"Something to watch. But in any case, tread lightly with just the basic information when you meet with Miriam. By the way, the missionary service committee has been calling the Minister's office, complaining about your lack of progress and saying that you are not communicating with them. I guess you'll make them sit up and take notice now. You better meet with them this afternoon to cool them off."

After calling Clayton Kratz, the chair of the committee, to set up an afternoon appointment at his hotel, Kingman went down to the front door to wait for his pickup by *Seguridad Pública.*

Carlos Rios had the full appearance of being Noriega's "top man." Bounding out of the rear seat of one of the shiny new blue cruisers, he greeted Rob with a smile, an extended hand, and a cheery *'Buenos Dias.'* Crisp green uniform, black moustache and hair – with gray showing at the temples, Captain Rios cut a professional figure. Kingman greeted him and sat in the rear seat of the patrol car.

Rios began in clear English, "When I called Miriam Voth an hour ago, she was quite upset that we were asking to visit her this morning. I just told her that we had made some progress in the investigation and that you, the

Canadian vice-consul, wanted to meet with her. But I think she suspects the worst."

"I won't go into any details about how he was found or how he left his car. By the way, are there any more details?"

"Nothing of consequence. We think that the situation with his car makes it likely he was covering his tracks for an affair. Maybe he ran into grief with someone who tried to roll him. More likely a jealous American lover."

Rob touched his head and looked out the window, feeling a bit alarmed.

Miriam Voth greeted them in front of her modest white washed cottage, set back amongst some palms in a middle class district. Her colorless face was torn with anguish and uncertainty. A few wisps of her sandy hair, which was done up in a severe bun, escaped from under a broad brimmed Panama hat. Two small children, Kate and Edwin, clutched anxiously at her plain cotton skirt. Their fair hair was bleached by the sun and many freckles dotted their faces and arms. They looked fearfully at the approaching men. Miriam invited them all into her cooler living room, where Anita, the maid, took away the reluctant children.

"I'm afraid Kevin's been found in the Canal Zone, dead," was all Kingman got out before Miriam Voth crumpled in her chair and began sobbing uncontrollably. Awkwardly, Kingman stood and moved towards her, placing his hand on her shoulder. She looked up, stood, and pulled herself into his chest, two fists up, shuddering with tears. After a few moments, Rob encircled her shoulders in his arms and then held her at a distance, looking into her tear-stained face.

After a few gasps, she said, "I'm sorry to be so weak. It's

just that... I hadn't dreamed he would be dead. Not really. Not Kevin... what will I tell the children?"

"It's a terrible shock," Rob said, inadequately. "Unfortunately I do have to ask you one more thing that will be very difficult. We need you to come to the morgue... to make a positive identification."

Breathing deeply and regaining her composure somewhat, Miriam said, "I suppose I will have to, won't I? I mean, I need to see him again, and-" she broke off sobbing.

During the trip to the morgue, Miriam sat stone-faced, staring out the window. After a seeming eternity, they turned in at the general hospital, a large complex of peeling white painted buildings amid rows of poorly tended palms. They entered a low annex at the rear of the compound. Her jaw was rigid, her eyes red, but dry. An attendant pushed through two massive swinging doors into a relatively cool examining room. A gurney, covered with a sheet stood in the middle and a strong smell of antiseptic assailed their nostrils. Rob's hand moved to his throat as he fought off a cough.

In contrast to her rigid stoicism when they arrived, Miriam hurled herself on his body when the sheet was pulled back and she saw him. With a throaty scream of grief and agony, she sobbed, "Kevin, no. Kevin, no..."

Back at the Hotel Panama later that afternoon, the four members of the committee filed into Kingman's meeting room. Expectation and demand was written on their severe faces. After a few minutes of preliminaries, he watched with guarded pleasure as their faces shifted from distain, to surprise, and then embarrassment.

"I found Kevin Voth face down in the mud in a swamp

in the Canal Zone. He had been stabbed in the back several times. The American Military Police are continuing their investigation and will report back. Meanwhile, his body has been transferred to the Panama General Hospital, where Miriam Voth has identified it positively. She has not been taking it well- of course, a major shock.

"I have not shared any of the following details with Mrs. Voth so that she would not speculate on any agonizing scenarios before the facts were known," Rob said. He paused a moment, and then he continued, somewhat louder than intended. "His abandoned car was discovered by *Seguridad Pública* near the *Zona Rosa*. His wedding ring and wallet were found locked in the glove compartment and the car had not been tampered with." He looked at each face around the table frozen now in disbelief with what they were hearing about a fellow missionary.

"This of course has lead Panamanian security to suggest that a clandestine affair was in progress. The investigation to determine the facts behind his death and find the culprit or culprits, is continuing. That is all I can tell you for now. When you are in contact with Miriam Voth, I would ask you for the present not to discuss these details with her. That will all come in good time."

At the end of the meeting, Rob rose and held open the door. The subdued committee members rose slowly and shuffled out. There was shame and confusion in their averted eyes and in their mumbled thanks. He guessed they would not be phoning the Minister's office for a time.

CHAPTER 4

Captain Rios was very thorough, as his appearance had suggested. Before dinner, he called Kingman at the hotel to tell him his colleagues had questioned the mission school director and had identified a certain student, whom Kevin Voth had been giving special private lessons to, as a person of interest. Did the vice-consul wish to accompany him to her apartment for an interview tomorrow morning?

As their bright blue patrol car surged from the hotel into the honking morning traffic heading West on *Via España*, and a soft waft of Rios' spicy cologne reached him and conquered the disgusting street smells, Rob turned to Captain Rios and wondered to himself how he managed to stay so well turned out.

"We're heading to *Casco Antiguo*, near the port, Balboa. It's an older area, where a lot of recent refugees from Chile and elsewhere have settled," said Rios in response to Rob's questioning look.

Shortly, they turned off *Avenida Central* onto a residential street lined with much older two and three storied yellow plastered *casas* with high windows and second floor balcony walkways. Rusting corrugated iron pitched roofs capped most of them, many badly in need of maintenance. The morning the sun shore brightly, making the whole street virtually steam with musty, pungent humidity.

After a repeated firm knock from Rios, Carmen Torres opened the door to her second floor flat. She was taller than Rob had expected, with gorgeous, cascading auburn hair, a straight nose, and beautiful olive skin. *Mestiza*, he thought.

"*Quién estan? Qué pasa?*" she demanded to know, her dark eyes smoldering with indignation at this intrusion into her life.

"*El capitán Ríos de Seguridad Pública, a su servicio, señorita, y este es el vicecónsul canadiense. Tenemos algunas preguntas que nos gustaría preguntarle en relación con el señor Kevin Voth.*"

Taken aback, she flushed deeply, but with the singular grace of a dancer, swept her arm to invite them in.

"*Si, accommodarse.*"

When they were seated, Rob asked, "How do you come to be in this *barrio*?" Looking somewhat reluctant and glancing at Rios, Carmen switched to very passable English for Rob's benefit.

"You know, my brothers and I came here as refugees from Colombia. There is terrible violence that took our parents who had a *hacienda* near Medellin that produced fruit. Those who came in jeeps with guns wanted it to grow *coca*. They simply took it over and sent my mother and father away when they tried to resist- they disappeared. We were allowed to flee. The authorities could do nothing. Later, we learned they were dead."

"So, how did you get to Panama?" queried Captain Rios.

"We just kept going and finally found a kind priest in Cartagena who took us in and told us about refuge here in

Panama. He helped us with the travel and to find this place to live. After some time I enrolled in another missionary school, where Kevin Voth taught."

"So, how long had you known Kevin?" asked Rob, a bit sharply.

"Almost a year now. For the past few months, I have been taking after hours lessons from him and now speak as you see."

"And your brothers, where are they?" asked Rios.

"I..., I haven't seen them since Kevin disappeared a few days ago," she explained hesitantly. "Until this last time, Pedro and Hernan always cleared out when Kevin came by for the English lesson. They work at a bar downtown. On his last visit, they stayed."

"They asked Kevin if he was married. At first, he said no, but then admitted he was, as the white ring around his otherwise sunburned ring-finger clearly indicated." Carmen smiled to herself at this point. " Then they asked, 'Why don't you see our sister at other times, take her out for dinner or an evening walk, or come to one of her concerts?' Kevin said he couldn't be free to do anything but give me English lessons."

Captain Rios shifted and coughed. Rob glanced across at him, eyes meeting knowingly.

"Then they said, 'Well, if you don't intend to live with her or marry her, you better not come here.' Kevin replied that his intentions were honorable. He was just giving her lessons. He could not do anything for now, but said... more could happen in the future. They were not convinced and asked him to come outside, because they wanted to talk to him some more. I asked them to wait, to settle this later.

Not to interfere. They refused. That was the last time I saw him, or Pedro and Hernan."

"Where are they now?" demanded Captain Rios.

"I don't know, really. They haven't been back, which is very strange. And they haven't called. I need them to accompany me. I sing on Saturday night in Club Floridita. Pedro plays guitar and Hernan base," replied Carmen anxiously. "I guess they must have told Kevin to stay away."

At this, Kingman lost his cool. "Would it help you to remember where they are if I told you Kevin is dead? He was found murdered, stabbed in the back and dumped in the Canal Zone!"

"Oh, *Dios, Dios, Dios*," screamed Carmen, rising. "No, no, no. It can't be!" Clutching her breast she collapsed.

At this, they rose and left, Kevin eying Rios questioningly. On the return drive to the Hotel Panama, Captain Rios said that Carmen Torres knew a lot more about her brothers than she was willing to let on. He would let her settle down a bit and interview her again. At the hotel lobby, Kingman parted with a smile and a cheerful mock salute, agreeing they would keep each other informed of progress.

He turned to the hotel dining room for his lunchtime debriefing with Jack Middleton. Jack was into his first beer at a table by the pool. He waved his pipe cheerily as Kingman joined him and sat down.

"That was very interesting," recounted Rob. "I've just been to see a beautiful young singer who is a person of interest in Kevin Voth's disappearance. Apparently, her two brothers took exception to Voth's private English tutoring, and all three disappeared after her last lesson, which they cut short. So, we can well assume the probable outcome."

"Looks like you're onto something," puffed Middleton. "Where to from here?"

"Captain Rios said he wasn't satisfied with what she told him about her brothers' disappearance, so I assume he'll be interviewing her further."

"Yeah, I would try to be there if I were you, Rob. The interviewing could go very wrong, get ugly... you know? *Securidad* will move quickly if they've decided the brothers are it, and Carmen knows that. You have to watch for the forces of darkness gathering. I don't think you can expect to see the process of justice unfold from Noriega's people as you might expect it to, despite his extensive CIA training... or maybe because of it."

At this point, the hotel manager, in a state of anxiety, approached Kingman. "*Señor, El Colonel Noriega* would like to see you in the lobby."

Surprised, Rob pushed back his chair and said, "Sorry Jack, looks like a summons. I have to go. If I'm not back in ten minutes, just ask them to charge your lunch to my room and I'll call you later. By the way, I seem to have stumbled on Kevin Voth's body in the Canal Zone, courtesy of my taxista. Tell you more later!" He left a stunned Middleton to nurse his beer.

Noriega greeted him cheerily in a small boardroom off the lobby, with two armed guards standing outside the door. "Will you have a bite of lunch with me? I have an important message to pass from the president."

Kingman said cautiously. "I was just having lunch with Middleton when you summoned me, so no. But what is the message?"

Manuel Noriega's face darkened and he scowled as he motioned for Kingman to sit. "Let's have *a café con leche*, anyways. We can't rush this."

He waived the hovering waiter away. "President Torrijos would like your ambassador to meet with him shortly to pass a special request from Panama to your minister."

"Can't you give me a little more to go on? I know it's the president who's making the request, but my ambassador will want a little more information about the request. You know, so he can background himself on the issue and give our minister a heads up before the request comes in. Maybe an *aide memoir*?" Kingman was thinking of Langman's dislike of surprises, especially if they put him in an awkward position in negotiations.

Noriega snorted. "This is important and high level, and my president wants nothing in writing at this point." He was almost shouting with impatience, face red, collar button about to burst. Breath coming in short gasps.

"You can assure Ambassador Langman that it will be worthwhile for him to come to Panama City to meet with President Torrijos!"

The knock on the door announced the arrival of the coffee, but Noriega rose and said shortly, "You'll let me know as soon as you get a reply from your ambassador, so I can make arrangements. You can assure him we will meet him at the airport and give him a proper reception with the president any time he can come, which I trust will be very soon."

With that, Noriega left, and Kingman hurried to his room to call San Jose.

"Well, some excitement at last," chortled Craig

Langman. "You don't suppose it has anything to do with the disappearance of our missionary friend?"

"Maybe incidentally," responded Kingman. "Though you never know. The Americans were very cooperative. Kind of took the steam out of any Noriega plan, if there was one. There could be some tie-in, but I can't see it now unless he is able to find an American to pin it on!

"I'm making some progress in that we seem to have tracked down a suspect, a beautiful student of Kevin Voth's, whose brothers seem to have had a role in Voth's demise. But, of course, they are nowhere to be found to answer questions.

"As I mentioned to you, Craig, Noriega has asked me to give you a request from President Torrijos for an urgent meeting. Evidently, he has some high level request to pass on to our foreign minister. He wouldn't be more specific, nor would he provide an *aide memoire*. Is this the way they do business in Latin America?"

"Not uncommon. Let Noriega know I'll come on the first COPA flight in the morning. I'll see you at the airport then!"

The ambassador was set to arrive early the next morning, and Kingman would meet him at the airport along with Noriega's escort. He called Noriega's office and left the message. After all this, Rob felt he was deserving of a drink, so went to the poolside bar for a Cuba Libre with lots of ice and double rum.

In the late afternoon, when he returned to his room to change for dinner, a small, dark chambermaid was turning down his bed and placing a night-time chocolate on the pillow. He paused in the open doorway and was looking askance at her. She turned and smiled, her round face cheerful and open.

"No, I don't mean to proposition you – I've got a message from Carmen, who desperately needs your help. Please, you have to come see her," she pleaded, her face clouding.

"Who are you?" Kingman thought of Carmen's brothers and what they did to the last foreigner in Carmen's life.

"You have to help. She has no one else. I am Carmen's neighbor. I saw the Securidad take her away this afternoon for questioning. She said you're her only hope. So please, I've asked Johnny to help. He's waiting in his taxi out front."

"Well, you better come with me, then," countered Kingman.

"Oh no, I can't. If hotel management or security sees me with you, I won't be around tomorrow," she said quietly, genuine fear reflected in her dark eyes.

CHAPTER 5

Captain Rios sat across from Carmen Torres. His usually kind face was stern and scowling that afternoon. The interrogation room in the basement of the Palacio de Justicia was dank and dark, except for a single shaded light bulb that hovered over them, motionless in the heat.

"We need you to remember where your brothers are, Carmen. Pedro and Hernan can't be far, and it's very important that we get in touch with them. You know, this is not an ordinary situation. You have to understand. A great deal is at stake for Panama. If we do not solve this murder shortly, political relations with Canada will suffer," he said.

"You need to tell your brothers that they must come forward. You know, even if they are responsible for Kevin Voth's murder, they will be treated fairly under the law. It could have been a question of honor for the family, which will result in much more minor penalties. So tell me, Carmen."

"I don't know anything. I don't know where they are. I don't know if they killed Kevin." Carmen bowed her head and averted her eyes, then looking directly into his. "Can't you see that I wouldn't have wanted that? I loved him."

"You loved, him! Well maybe you loved too many foreigners. What about a certain American MP," Rios sneered, "where does he fit in your string of lovers?"

"I don't know what you are talking about. Wait, there has been a young American soldier who comes to the Club Floridita. Is he what you refer to as my string of lovers? I have spoken to him once, maybe twice, not more than that."

"You are trying to say you have never gone further than that with the blond man from Detroit? That he wasn't jealous of Kevin? Jealous enough to want him out of the way?"

"What? I have never given this soldier you describe any encouragement, though he may have asked. I don't recall."

Suddenly, Rios pushed back and stood, his normally controlled professional face contorted with rage as he spat out, "So remember where Pedro and Hernan are. You had no say in what happened to Voth? Tell me about your American lover! No?"

"I have nothing to say," Carmen pleaded, looking into Rios' eyes.

"Your time for speaking is up. You will be punished until you remember!" he spat.

With that, Rios left and was presently replaced in the interrogation room by two more junior guards, short, unkempt, and reeking of sweat and liquor.

They moved menacingly towards Carmen, who stood up. One got close, his face in hers, his foul breath almost choking Carmen, "where are your brothers?"

He slapped her. Hard. Completely surprised, Carmen fell backwards onto the floor. They grabbed her roughly by the shoulders, hoisting her to her feet. The one, standing in front of her, unbuckled his uniform trousers, while the other pulled her backwards onto the interview table. The second threw up her bright cotton skirt and tore off her panties as she struggled.

Carmen screamed and struggled, while the second guard held her down and slapped her. He pinned her shoulders harder down on the table with her arms wrenched up roughly over her head, until she lay still.

"Tell us, whore, and this will stop. Tell us, before my friend gets his turn," El Toro panted through clenched teeth. But she had nothing to tell them.

The guard called "El Toro" went first.

Neighbors' shutters slammed shut in the late afternoon heat as the bright blue *Policia Secreta* car arrived. Two *Seguridad* officers pulled her, staggering, up the outside stairs to her second floor flat. Bruised face and blood on her legs, they threw her through the front door of her apartment, where she crumpled onto the floor, weeping.

Through the open door they shouted, "You'd better tell your brothers we will be back tomorrow to see if your memory has improved!" They slammed the door, and Carmen was left heaped on the floor in the semidarkness of the deepening evening.

CHAPTER 6

The usually teeming street was still deserted two hours later as Johnny eased his taxi in to park in front of the two-storey plastered building. Eyes followed Kingman and Johnny through semi-closed shutters as they walked up the stairs to the second floor. It was eerily quiet as Rob raised his arm and knocked, then grabbed the doorknob and swung open the door. His hand went to his mouth. He gasped at Carmen's slouched figure on the floor in the dim doorway at the back of the room, her head resting on the frame.

"My God, Carmen, what happened?" He could smell the blood before he reached her. Instinctively he put out his arms, but Carmen shrank away.

"Don't touch me. I'm dirty." Carmen's hand went to cover her face as she looked up into Rob's eyes. Humiliation was written on a face that was twisted in pain. Bruises had appeared on her cheek and around her eye, and her bottom lip was torn. "They hurt me because I couldn't tell them where my brothers are," she managed slowly. "They'll be back tomorrow to ask again. But I don't know."

"You have to take Carmen with you, *Señor*," squeaked a fearful voice behind them. It was the chambermaid from the hotel. "They will be back tomorrow... and they will kill her... if she is here."

"Which 'they' are you talking about?" demanded Kingman, as he whirled with an aggressive step forward, fists clenched at his sides.

The girl shrank back.

"Captain Rios took me to an interrogation room at *Seguridad Publica* this afternoon," mumbled Carmen.

"Rios?" repeated Rob incredulously. He turned back to face Carmen, who spoke slowly.

"At first he was kind, but when I told him I didn't know where my brothers were, he left. Two others came and beat me and raped me and dumped me back here. They said they would be back tomorrow, and that I better know where my brothers are by then."

"She needs to see a doctor," pleaded tiny chambermaid, Maria, who by now was moving to the rear of the flat to pack a soft bag with meagre essentials and some clothing for Carmen.

"But you can't take her to the hospital, because all is reported to *Seguridad Publica*. Can the British consulate help?"

Kingman was at sea. He had grave doubts as they bundled a reluctant but compliant Carmen into the back seat of Johnny's taxi and headed for via España, but he could think of no alternative. The hotel was not safe and had no protection for Carmen from Panamanian security. Neither were the hospitals, which were obliged to report unusual situations.

After several minutes, Johnny lurched to a stop in front of the Chase Manhattan Bank building, where the British Embassy was located, just across from the Hotel Panama.

An armed guard in green *Seguridad* fatigues stood menacingly in front of the lobby door.

"Qué desea, señor?La Embajada está cerrada." "What do you want, mister? The Embassy is closed." He stood stolidly, blocking the way.

Kingman struggled to produce his diplomatic passport. *"Yo soy el vicecónsul canadiense. Tengo que tomar esta mujer en el consulado para una reunión."* "I'm the Canadian Vice-consul. I need to take this woman to the British Embassy for a meeting."

"Qué?" el guardia dijo dudosamente. "Por qué la Embajada Británica, si usted es canadiense? Es ella canadiense?" "What?" the guard said doubtfully. "Why the British Embassy if you are Canadian? Is she Canadian?"

" Ella necesita atención médica y estoy tratando de ayudarla. " "She needs medical attention and I am trying to protect her."

" Por qué no llevarla a un hospital? Te ayudaré." "Why not take her to a hospital? I will help you."

By this time, Johnny had appeared from behind. He held up his taxi licence to the guard and raising his rank, he asked, *" Sargento , es necesario llevarla a la Embajada porque un médico está llegando a verla. "* "Sergeant, it is necessary to take her into the Embassy because a doctor is coming to see her."

Reluctantly the guard pulled open the lobby door as Kingman nodded and pushed by, his arm around a stumbling Carmen. He pressed the night service button, and in a few long moments the elevator whirred and the British night guard stepped into the lobby.

Rob proffered his Diplomatic passport and explained

the seriousness of the predicament.

"You can't seriously expect me to let you in after hours with that baggage on board," the British night clerk sneered caustically in Carmen's direction. "It's against regulations. I'll go up and give Middleton a call... if you'd like. Wait here." With that, he was gone.

Rob looked around in the glaring fluorescent light for a spot to let Carmen sit down. A wooden desk stood vacant at the end of the elevator lobby and a row of plastic chairs rested against the side wall. The green clad Panamanian guard stared curiously through the glass doors, one hand on the sub machinegun slung across his chest. He turned and stepped back into a small guard box and bent down. Rob assumed he was calling *Seguridad*.

The British night guard returned. Middleton would be along shortly. They went up to the security of the waiting area in the Embassy.

When Middleton arrived, the Embassy doctor was summoned and Carmen was examined, stitched, given a shot of penicillin, and lay on the cot in the Embassy sick room. Middleton was clearly not happy. He spoke in an agitated voice, out of Carmen's earshot.

"Well isn't this a fix? They obviously treated her very badly during the interrogation you say. We'll keep her here overnight and feed and water her, but you'll have to get her out first thing in the morning. She's not a British citizen or a Canadian, and we can't give her the protection of the Embassy without causing a major row with Noriega. What are you going to do? I assume she is the prime suspect you mentioned at lunch, though she looks a lot worse for wear?"

Rob nodded his assent to Middleton's statement and turned.

"The only thing I could think of for the short-term was to bring her here. She said *Seguridad* would be back for more questioning tomorrow. The hotel isn't safe. She says she's a refugee, but has no documentation, though she wouldn't even if that were true. I don't know what to believe or not believe about her past. But one thing's for sure, if we leave her at her flat, she could be dead by sundown tomorrow. Not only will we never unravel the involvement of her brothers in Voth's demise, Jack, but... I can't believe the brutality of the administration of justice here." Rob shook his head.

"Don't say I didn't warn you. But it does surprise me that they would act so openly. You'd better call your ambassador on the secure line and get his advice. We seem to be up against it, and you'll need his support, whichever way you jump," proffered Middleton.

"He'll be particularly pleased to hear from me at this time of night when he's trying to get to bed early for his flight here first thing in the morning. Noriega has asked him to come in to meet with President Torrijos. Seems there's something big in the wind." Middleton's eyebrows rose.

Craig Langman was, to say the least, not overjoyed to receive the midnight briefing from Kingman on the status of the murder and Carmen Torres.

"My God, man, you can't take on Noriega. At some point, he'll fail to grant you diplomatic immunity, especially where the woman is concerned. You said she's not a Canadian Citizen, or even documented as a refugee, is she?"

"No, Craig, but she *is* a refugee. Even more so now. We have to get her to Costa Rica, or they'll kill her."

"Well, she is definitely a refugee from violence, and it's obvious the state won't protect her - they are the perpetrators. But, technically, she hasn't yet made a refugee application to us. Legally we're in no man's land. See if Middleton has some kind of a refugee application form, fill it out, and have him fax it to us in San Jose. That will give us a toe-hold in the process. The rest we'll discuss tomorrow morning when I get there."

"Oh, make sure you and the woman both carry copies of the document with you when you cross the border into Costa Rica. It's flimsy, and you'll probably have to bluff your way through, but it's better than nothing. Be careful; if you're caught, the Panamanians are likely to view it as aiding a fugitive from justice... We'll talk again when I see you in the morning. Good luck."

CHAPTER 7

Captain Rios was waiting for Rob in the lobby of the Hotel Panama when he returned late. At that moment, he was the last person Rob wanted to see.

"What the hell are you doing here?" Rob nearly shouted.

"Thought I would drop by to give you a little friendly advice," said Rios evenly, without any hint of a smile. "We will seek out Carmen Torres when she leaves the British Embassy. She is witness to a murder and perhaps an accessory. We will arrest her and interrogate her."

Anger welled up in Rob's voice as he went up on his toes, fists clenched by his sides, towering over Rios, "Haven't you done enough interrogation? Your methods are unusually brutal, and well beyond the law."

"*Señor* Kingman, you don't understand lefty Latinas. They will never talk unless you use harsh methods. You are in Latin America now, so leave your Boy Scout mentality back in Canada. Don't you see that it is in your interest to bring the perpetrators of this murder to justice? Think of Miriam and her children."

"I don't believe what I'm hearing from you, Captain Rios. Good night." With that, Rob spun on his heel and made his way briskly towards the elevators and his room.

Rob called Sophie at home in San Jose, waking her late

to recount the day's startling events, with anger and fury mounting in his voice.

"Take it easy, Rob. I know it seems harsh to say, but I don't want you to take all that risk to get this refugee out. I just need you to come home safely before the baby is born.

"By the way, Rob, did you remember that Jim and Belinda Lovett were sailing down from the British Virgin Islands to see us in Costa Rica? They called today from a marina in Colón where they are moored taking on supplies. They'll be sailing up the Panamanian coast to Limon. You can probably get them there tomorrow, if you call the marina. They left me the number."

Rob thoughtfully jotted down the number remembering that the hotel was probably eavesdropping on his calls. He would give the Lovetts a call and see if he could meet them the following evening. A plot was already hatching in his mind when he signed off with love and assurances to Sofia that he would be home very soon.

Jim Lovett was an old university friend and a former colleague who had quit the Foreign Service the year before, after an unsatisfactory first posting in Australia. His pugnacious nature and strongly held views did not seem to be compatible with the older, conservative ambassador he came up against. So, he turned to living his dream of sailing the Caribbean and writing books. And his wife, Belinda, became a fine sailor even though she was from the prairies.

Rob smiled to himself as he remembered Jim's eulogies over endless whiskey sours, about the exploits of Joshua Slocum, a Nova Scotian who was the first to sail single-handedly around the world in the late nineteenth Century.

Rob sweated and tossed and turned on his hotel room bed in the dark. Sleep wouldn't come. Middleton's questions swirled in his mind. Would the Americans help to get her out? Probably not, with the situation in the Canal Zone as it was. What grounds could he argue, as he really knew next to nothing about her? Was she complicit in Kevin's murder? She'd said she loved him, so probably not. Did she know where her brothers were? Was Rob blinded by compassion and getting played? He could easily end up in serious, career-ending trouble if he got her out of Panama and maybe worse if he failed. He was risking a great deal with Sophie in her condition. It all seemed a high-risk dead end.

CHAPTER 8

Rob's meeting with Ambassador Langman at Tocumen airport in the morning did not go at all as expected. As he paced in the VIP lounge the COPA plane taxied up. A large black limousine followed by two security vehicles pulled up to the foot of the aircraft stairs. Noriega emerged from the back seat and greeted Ambassador Langman, and then pulled him into the car.

Rob watched, too late to push out onto the tarmac. As he strode urgently toward the security guard's kiosk to ask to be let out, Langman was whisked away to the meeting with President Torrijos without so much as a glance in Rob's direction.

Rob anxiously awaited the delivery of the ambassador's suitcase to the VIP lounge and then went out to find Johnny, who was still waiting for a fare at the front of the terminal. They headed for the British Embassy to see Middleton, but more importantly for Rob, to see how Carmen had made it through the night.

Jack Middleton was quite agitated as he greeted Rob. "Noriega's on to us. I was just about to turn Carmen Torres over to *Seguridad Publica* and put you out of your misery. Out of danger too, I might add. Do I see in your eyes a risky scheme brewing?"

"Well, Jack," Rob said, alarmed at Middleton's apparent callous indifference, "since Carmen doesn't seem to have much prospect here with you or with *Seguridad Publica,* I'll have to try and make other arrangements. Can I use your phone?"

The call to the marina in Colón was encouraging, but not completely satisfactory. The marina manager promised to deliver a message to the Lovitts, whose sloop, Gypsy Moon, was moored offshore. The marina was not sure when they would be setting sail, but knew it was soon, as they were provisioning the boat. The message Rob left for them was that he would come to see them and tour their boat that afternoon.

As Rob's taxi headed down the Isthmian highway for the thirty five mile trip to Colón, Johnny glanced nervously in the rear view mirror at the blue Seguridad Publica tail they had acquired.

"One de' new Dodge Darts. *Policia Segreta!*" he said with a frown. "Gonna be trouble."

Ships crossing through the canal to the Pacific start on the Caribbean side at the twin cities of Cristobol and Colón. One merges into the other almost imperceptibly, with both being built on Manzanillo Island, at the entrance to the canal, now joined to the mainland. Colón was founded in 1852 as the terminus of the railway across the Isthmus. Cristobol came into being as the port of entry for the supplies used in building the canal and was now the second largest city in Panama.

Despite fine public buildings, hospitals, theaters, and well-stocked shops, Colón had some of the nastiest slums in Latin America and was generally dirty as befits a port city. It was not a healthy place for an evening stroll, though full of cabarets and places of pleasure. They passed the beautiful cathedral, a bust of de Lesseps, and a statue of Columbus. They headed out Marine Drive along the waterfront, all the while their blue security tail intact.

Rob hailed Jim and Belinda on their boat moored offshore to a buoy, who soon launched their dinghy and greeted him on the dock with much backslapping and warm embraces.

"Our Man in Panama!" shouted Jim enthusiastically, "What a treat to see you! Let's head out to Gypsy Moon and catch up over a beer." Johnny elected to stay on shore and look after his taxi, though he was sure nothing would happen to it with the security detail parked in full view.

"We have orders to keep the vice-consul safe," was all they said when Johnny wandered over casually to ask.

"Gypsy Moon is a forty-five foot, center cockpit cruising yacht. Set up with two staterooms and two masts, she's also well-equipped for navigation," Jim offered proudly over the roar of the small outboard. "She has a brand new eighty-five horsepower Yanmar diesel engine and five sails. Passage was easy from the British Virgin Islands, island-hopping through the Windwards, then finally via Margarita Island off the Venezuelan coast. We had a great time getting here."

Onboard, Jim was effusive in his praise of the handling qualities and speed of the ship. Belinda, who normally served as captain, could hardly get a word in. She hugged Rob and pushing a strand of her sun-streaked blond hair out of her eyes, she turned to Jim.

"Cool it, Jim. Maybe Rob would like a beer. There's a nice

breeze, so let's sit back in the cockpit, under the sunshade." She smiled as she brushed sexily past Rob to head down into the cabin, reminding him of their university days.

Well into his second beer, Rob outlined the particular difficulty he was in.

"Carmen Torres may well be the prime suspect, but beating and rape was over the top as an interrogation method. Poor woman is standing up well, but we really have to get her out of Noriega's clutches if she is going to have any real chance at justice. She's suffered a lot as a refugee from Colombia, and now she doesn't have a future here!"

As Rob had hoped, Jim was outraged at the injustice, and full of adventure and bravado.

"Well, we sure are willing to help. Can't believe how she's been treated." Jim took an incensed swill of his beer. "We can get her up to Costa Rica, anyways; and you can take it from there."

"The problem will be how to get Carmen on board Gypsy Moon, with the security detail that I seem to have acquired. How about I try to figure out a way to lose them and deliver her to Portobello, a few hours up the coast? Can you meet us there tonight?"

"Sure, let me see," Jim said, examining a coastal chart. "Yeah. We can motor up after midnight. Anchor in the bay. If the coast is clear, you can signal from one of the old for- tifications with a flashlight. I'll pick her up in the dinghy and then sail off to Puerto Limon in Costa Rica."

"Hold it. Maybe better if we meet up in Cahuita Bay, forty miles south of the city so we avoid complications with immigration in Puerto Limon. She doesn't have much for papers. You'll have to watch for the huge coral reef that provides the breakwater for Cahuita Bay." The plan had been hatching in Rob's mind much of the day.

"Sounds like a challenge," beamed Jim." We can finish provisioning and sail the thirty miles northeast from here to Portobello by early morning, so we've got a plan."

Belinda, who would be doing most of the tricky night-time sailing, was not as enthusiastic. But they shook hands and embraced warmly, Belinda getting her hugs too. They worked their way down the rear ladder to the waiting dinghy.

Johnny was somewhat fearful, rolling his eyes at the arrangements Rob had made, but the taxista soon had a plan for giving the slip to *Seguridad* for the night time trip to Portobello.

CHAPTER 9

Just after dark, Derek, Johnny's younger brother, pulled up to the rear service entrance of the British Embassy building, opened the door, and stepped down from his dark blue delivery van. Of stocky build, he moved athletically to the rear of his van and opened the doors. Glancing round, he paused to breathe in the humid night air and listened intently for approaching vehicles through the chorus of cicadas. He carried two empty cardboard boxes up the platform steps and rang the service entrance buzzer. The door swung open from the inside and Derek stepped in.

"The guard's no longer lookin' down the side of the buildin', so you climb in front, quick."

Two shadowy figures hurried around the front of the van, opened the passenger door and climbed between the seats onto an old mattress spread on the floor in back. The air was stifling as Carmen and Rob settled down on the musty mattress, their backs against opposite walls of the otherwise bare van.

"So far, so good," Rob muttered under his breath as Derek opened the driver's door, sat in, and backed out onto the street.

Rob touched his thigh where he felt pain. He lowered his right leg to the mattress, relieving the discomfort caused by the Webley semi-automatic pistol in his right pocket, which was jammed uncomfortably into his thigh. Middleton had thrust the old gun into his hand at the last moment and stepped away.

Rob was most uncomfortable with the prospect of using a gun. Not that he wasn't familiar with them; he'd grown up on a farm, and had even become a champion sharpshooter in his Air Cadet squadron during high school. But this was different. He took the pistol out of his pocket and laid it on the musty mattress beside him.

Carmen's eyes widened and went from the gun to his face. She said in a low voice, vibrating with the rough ride of the van, "We're not going to use that, are we?"

"No. I'm going to leave it there for Derek to return to Middleton."

Rivulets of sweat ran down the back of Rob's neck as the van turned onto the Isthmian highway to Colón.

Johnny, with his girlfriend as decoy sitting beside him in his taxi, had preceded them down the highway by about fifteen minutes, security detail intact. As Derek accelerated down the nearly deserted-highway, he shouted back that there seemed to be no one following them. Rob settled back against the wall of the van and relaxed a bit.

Carmen smiled at him in the semidarkness, then, flashing oncoming headlights lit up her face as she winced at the pain from her split lip. Rob's heart went out to her, and he reached for her, remembering what she had been through in the last day and a half. He wanted to move to put his arm around her in the semidarkness of the van, but thought better of it and stopped. He knew she was very sore in many places and his awkward efforts in the lurching van would likely not be a comfort. He hoped that the road ahead to Portobello would not be too rough. It was a fabled town as he had learned from the guide-book.

Portobello lay some thirty miles northeast of Colón by sea and by road. Columbus used the harbor in 1502. It was a Spanish garrison town for more than two centuries. Sir Francis Drake died and was buried at sea off the Bay of Portobello. Three large stone forts guard the entrance to the harbour with old Spanish cannon. Gold from Peru was brought over the trail from Panama City and stored in the treasure house until the galleons from Spain arrived.

In the cathedral is a statue of the Black Christ; it was being shipped from Spain to the viceroy of Peru, but the ship was wrecked in the bay and sank. Later, the statue was salvaged by the locals. The image is paraded through the streets of the old town at nightfall on this very day in October; afterwards there is feasting and dancing till dawn.

The partying was well underway as the little van turned east off the Panama City highway at Sabanitas, just before Colón, onto the Portobello Road and began the hour's journey to their destination.

The van skidded slightly as Derek swerved off the pavement and onto the gravel track. Its dim headlights were aided by the bright waxing moon which illuminated the narrow ribbon of road stretching through the deep tropical forest.

"This gonna be some drive," shouted Derek, hitting the brakes and swerving again to miss a surprised tapir taking a dust bath in the warm gravel.

"We got lots of other critters to watch out for, like pumas, jaguar, peccary, deer, wild hog, ocelots - tigrillos...

Hope we don't get a flat tire or run outta gas." He grinned mischievously, glancing in the rear view mirror for a reaction. But there wasn't one.

Shortly, they came to an open area, a banana plantation. Carmen spoke up somewhat plaintively, "I really need to pee; can we stop here?"

Derek pulled up, and said, "Wait till I get out and look around to make sure there's nuttin' about. Don't go gettin'off t' road, an' watch for coral snakes."

"Si, I'll be careful. I come from the banks of the Orinoco."

Rob opened the back doors cautiously and stepped down onto the gravel and moved towards the ditch for a similar mission. Shadows of banana plants stood still in the blackness. He could see Carmen's silhouette in the moonlight a few steps away and heard her groan in pain as she crouched on the gravel, skirt hiked up to her hips. He could only imagine the searing pain she must have been feeling and went over to help her up. He lifted her by both arms. She rose unsteadily and leaned briefly into his embrace on the moonlit road. Amongst the cicada chorus, they could hear an ocelots' screeching hunting cry somewhere in the forest, and she trembled despite the warm night air.

Derek shuffled and coughed beside the silent van, and said, "we best be on our way."

The journey to Portobello took somewhat longer than they had anticipated. Derek slowed, as they frequently encountered wildlife crossing the road. Eventually, the blinking lights of the port town came into view. Once in the town, the van crept slowly through throngs of revellers, until they parked it near the central square. It was nearing midnight. They could see flower petals strewn on the ceremonial parade route that had been trampled and scattered by the hundreds of finely dressed dancers.

The solemn parade had been led by little angels in puffy white embroidered blouses and skirts, strewing flower petals from baskets, followed by priests with tall crosses, chanting and swinging burning incense censors. Then came the robed men carrying the Black Christ on their shoulders from the port to its home in the Cathedral on the central square.

Many country folk accompanied them, shuffling along as conquistadors, Inca Kings, warrior priests, and some wearing European faces and clothes. Next were Mayan forest spirits sporting Jaguar masks and local Indian costumes, and others with fierce Amazonian style paint and feather headdresses.

Only moments before the van's arrival at the outskirts, a big papier mache devil Judas was burnt in the central square. A heap of ashes and a wire frame was all that remained as the dance of the dirty little devils began. Shortly after this dancing drama of the Montezumas reached its frenzied peak, it was replaced by guitars strumming folk tunes that invited dance.

Now the square was alive with drums everywhere, beating out syncopated Latin rhythms. The music was cheerful, optimistic, the contagious beats of Africa blended with the melodic tones and dance steps of Andalusia. Fierce Jaguar faces could still be seen, but mainly it was couples dancing now. A hoarse song was sung by dancing women, clapping in the air, turning to show appealing figures. Bystanders clapped and swayed in time with the music. Everyone moved rhythmically.

The mejorana, a folk dance to the music of native guitars began, with its laments of the *gallo* (rooster), *gallina* (hen), and *zapatero* (shoemaker). Then it gave way to the sensuous beat of the *cumbia*. Dancers exchanged lighted candles, looking suggestively into each other's eyes and strutting high, or clapping and circling each other in anticipation of trysts.

Carmen by this time was clapping and swaying, her body beautiful in its sinuous movements. Exhaustion and pain overcome for the moment, she turned to Rob and shouted hoarsely, "This is the soul of my people!" She reached for him with two hands.

Time stood still as the passionate rhythmic dancing swept them up. Rob felt the deep and passionate rhythm of all around him. Yet, he was confused by his feelings and thought about Sofia and their baby. In a short while, it came back to him why they found themselves there, and he remembered the brutality Carmen was fleeing. He grabbed Carmen's upper arms, held her still, and looked around to see if he could find Derek.

He shouted, "We have to go!" She nodded, her bold smile still lighting up her face as she clutched Rob's hand. They threaded their way through the dancers to the darkened street at the edge of the Plaza, where they found Derek beside the van.

As the van eased through the crowds towards the port, a large Spanish colonial fortress loomed out of the darkness, outlined in the moonlight, watchful over the beautiful bay. Ramparts rose thirty feet, topped with crenellated battlements. Time blackened cannons faced the sea. The excitement of old battles seemed to float on the air.

Derek parked the truck in the moon shadow of the Fort. As they climbed towards the ramparts, Rob said quietly, "I don't see the boat yet, but it's early. Not yet two."

He stopped and held up his watch for Carmen to see in the moonlight. She glanced at it distractedly, flipping her hair and wiping the nape of her neck with her hand.

Derek rustled behind them, "I'll go get some food. Saw a roti vendor some ways back." They nodded assent and then sat, half lying on the cool grass, propped against the battlements near a cannon port with a good view of the harbour. Rob could feel her warm body pressing beside his and smelled her scent from the dance.

"This has been such a wonderful night. I don't want to leave. My brothers are here – what will I do?" She looked up into his face.

"Carmen, it's too dangerous to stay. We'll have to figure out your next steps from Costa Rica. The authorities are not goons. You will be protected."

"You are so kind, just like Kevin was," she said. "But what about money? Where will I stay?"

"We'll work it out. I've sent an application forward for our refugee program. While you're waiting, I don't know... maybe you can sing in a club, make money. I'll meet you in Cauhita after Jim and Belinda sail you there. Don't worry. I'll take care of you."

"God, what leaps you make. What are your friends like on the boat? Why are they doing this? What will your wife say when she sees me?"

Before Rob could reply, two shadowy figures loomed over them, brandishing knives. With a face contorted in anger, one spat "Hey, gringo," kneeling and pressing the knife to Rob's throat. "Maybe I should cut your throat. You got money? Passport? Hand it over!" Rob struggled to stand, but the mugger forced him down, back to the stone ramparts.

The other, lewdly pressing into Carmen's face, threatened, "You got something else I want, Chica, hot from the dance!"

Suddenly a deafening report and a blue flash ripped through the tropical sky.

"Get outta' here, you bastards, or you' dead!"

Without a glance around, the two hooligans fled.

Derek lowered his arm and thrust the Webley into his belt, smiling broadly. "Pretty chicken shit, eh? Anyone for goat rotis and ginger beer?"

Carmen sobbed loudly with relief, her hands to her face, her chest heaving. Rob jumped up and tightly embraced Derek.

"Oh shit, man. That was close. Thank you."

They turned towards the harbor. They could hear the soft throbbing of Gypsy Moon's diesel engine, her prow cutting through the quiet water, and see her red and green navigation lights blinking into view.

The boat dropped anchor a hundred yards offshore. Derek flashed the signal torch toward it. It was only a few minutes later that Jim's dinghy crunched into the rocky shingle on the beach beside the fortress.

"Thank God you're here, Jim."

"Didn't we hear a shot?"

"There's no time for chat. We're expecting official visitors any moment. This is Carmen Torres. Good luck. I'll meet you in Cahuita Bay in what, four or five days?"

Jim took her bag and then her hand, steadying her climb over the gunwale of the small craft as he stood in the water.

"Yes, if the weather holds," Jim said breathlessly as he climbed in after the bag. Rob pushed off the dinghy from shore, "take care and see you then."

Reaching the idling sloop, engine burbling softly in the moonlight, Carmen clambered out of the dingy and over the stern. Jim followed with her bag. Belinda, with a heavily gloved hand, wound the windlass to ship the anchor chain on the bow deck. She turned quickly and strode to the helm. In one deft motion, she shifted into forward and pushed the idling diesel's throttle home.

After watching Belinda head for open water, Rob and Derek turned around to return to the van, only to find themselves face to face with two local policemen who had come up silently behind them, with guns drawn.

"Who's doin' the shootin'?" they demanded.

"Boss was attacked by hooligans with knives. I fired in the air to scare 'em off, that's all. Then the other couple left on their boat after the fiesta."

Unbelieving, one cop reached for the old automatic tucked in Derek's belt, while the other covered him. "This the gun?" Then, he said to Rob, "Lemme' me see your passport, gringo."

By this time, Gypsy Moon had ascribed an arc, deftly navigating among other anchored yachts in the Bay, and was now heading for the open Caribbean.

"You better come down to the station and we'll make a few phone calls, *señores*," one said, "we'll have to hold you until we get things straightened out."

"Look," Rob said, shaking his passport at them, "I'm a diplomat, and there is going to be trouble if you take me off to jail."

"So what? Somebody's shootin'. We're the law here, and we gotta do our job."

"Isn't there a fine or something we could pay?" said Derek, cocking his head aside. "Boss here has to catch a plane in Panama City early tomorrow."

Rob reached for his wallet, as the cop watched cautiously, gun still levelled.

"How much ya got? A hundred ought to do it, for disturbing' the peace," smiled the elder, as Rob proffered two fifties, "but we're still keepin' the gun and makin' calls."

In a short while Rob and Derek were heading out of town in the van, minus Middleton's automatic and the hundred dollars. Rob shuddered to think what would have come to pass if the two cops had arrived minutes earlier, with Carmen still on the shore.

CHAPTER 10

Sophie reached up and wiped her neck as she sat flushed and hot in the driver's seat of the family Peugeot station wagon, parked at the curb in front of La Sabana airport. She watched distractedly as a short Costa Rican gentleman walked his dog on a leash between the palm trees on the Boulevard. She tried to subdue her irritation over Rob's delayed return from Panama City, where he had no doubt put himself in danger, but continued to nurse the sense of desertion she had developed through what had been a difficult week.

She put her hand on her swelling tummy, more obvious now in the later stages. How rotten she had felt in the mornings in the early stages of her pregnancy. She felt pleased that she had managed to carry on with her work with the children of the Santa Ana orphanage in the far south of the city, traveling there in a sweltering, crowded bus every other morning, risking the motion sickness that plagued her.

Many of the babies were small and subdued, crying pitifully for love and attention from their attendants. Abandoned at birth and consequently slow developmentally, they were now returning her affection and showed improvement. Sophie worried that some of the dire tropical infections they suffered would be passed on to her own baby.

And there had been the more threatening confrontations with her drunken and aggressive neighbour, Don Rodrigo Keith, head of the Costa Rican railways. Her Siamese cat had been prowling the adjoining wall nocturnally, howling loudly in heat. Don Rodrigo seemed to enjoy returning Taja and drawing out his long complaints laced with sexual innuendos, while at the same time leering at her beautiful young body, now showing clearly the signs of the coming baby.

Workers on the street sucked in their breath as she walked by and almost inaudibly threw gentle taunts of *"Mamacita"* (Little Momma), *"Chica caliente, venga conmigo!* (Hot chickie, come with me)," and *"Aie, que guapa!* (Wow, how gorgeous!)" She was in the full bloom of womanhood with the added exotic attraction of long blonde hair and blue eyes. Her eyes flashed as a hand brushed back some hair. She was angry with Rob for not being there at her side to deflect their unwanted attentions.

Rob burst through the glass doors of the terminal, suitcase in hand. Sophie rose from the driver's seat to greet him, bumping her tummy painfully on the steering wheel. At the same time, adding to her annoyance, the diminutive Costa Rican man walking his dog was headed straight for them, and in fact now seemed to address her as he approached.

"I couldn't help but notice your diplomatic license plates. I'm Pepe Figueras," he said more to Rob, who by now was approaching the rear of the car. Rob towered over him, but managed with singular grace to set down his case and reach up to the boulevard to shake the proffered hand.

"Mucho gusto, Señor Presidente! Oltra ves," Rob said, which caused Sophie to open her mouth in amazement. Recovering, she quickly extended her hand and also smiled down into his face, hiding her astonishment that such a diminutive man could be Costa Rica's much fabled revolutionary president.

Both Rob and the president couldn't help staring at Sophie, whose skimpy cotton dress with its red and yellow flowers left little to the imagination.

"Y Señora, mucho gusto!" proffered President Figueres, bowing to kiss her hand, which drew another very becoming flush to Sophie's face.

"A pleasure to meet you, sir," Sophie said, withdrawing her hand and removing her sunglasses.

Figueres grasped her hand warmly again, and, holding it, went on, "You Canadians are looking quite at home here. Costa Rica is not really a country, you know; it's more of a pilot project!" He continued to stare into her eyes causing her to flush again. He turned and winked at Rob.

"Yes, we're quite enjoying life here," Rob offered uncomfortably. With that, the president turned suddenly and strode to greet a woman looking very much like his wife, who was coming briskly, and with obvious annoyance, out of the terminal.

Rob and Sophie mumbled goodbyes and tumbled quickly into their car and sped off toward San Jose.

"Latin men! What was that all about?" demanded Sophie, now that she had caught her breath and was focusing again on Rob's absence and return.

"Well, I've met him on several occasions since my

presentation of credentials last year, so I assumed he was just being friendly," chatted Rob, glad of the distraction. "That comment about Costa Rica being a pilot project was just part of another conversation we had about development assistance some weeks back."

"Did you see how he looked at me? I can't stand the leering I've been getting from Costa Rican men of all levels and stripes while you've been away. You'd think a pregnant woman would be granted a little respect. Anyways, I am glad you're back – none too soon, as you can see!" Sophie glanced sideways at Rob, the flush rising up her cheeks, as her arm held her hair off the back of her neck.

"Let's go to Hotel Del Rio in the Orosi Valley for a lunch treat, Rob. I do need some care and feeding."

Despite his fatigue, Rob happily threaded his way through the light morning traffic across the North end of San Jose. Then he headed south down the highway to Cartago, the old capital that was destroyed in an earthquake years ago. Despite Sophie's magnetic allure beside him, he was still recounting anxiously to himself Carmen Torres' harrowing escape of the night before on Jim and Belinda's boat.

"...really well beyond the normal call of duty, I should say. What did the ambassador think?"

Sophie's comment snapped him back to the present, and he realized he had not been following the veiled complaints she had been making about his delayed arrival from Panama. With a flush, he managed, "Noriega whisked him off to a meeting with President Torrijos when he arrived at the airport, so I really didn't have the opportunity to consult before her escape. We'll see what he thinks when

I meet with him Monday morning. Jim and Belinda will sail up to Cauhita near Limon. You remember, where we met the old fisherman David living on the beach, and went snorkeling to see the beautiful fish on the reef. Claude and I'll go to meet them and bring Carmen back to San Jose." He smiled. She nodded hesitantly, frowning.

"Bring Carmen here, eh? Should I be jealous?" demanded Sophie suspiciously. "And I really didn't expect you would put Jim and Belinda in so much danger!"

"No, look Sweetheart. What else could I do? While being a prime suspect in Kevin Voth's murder, she was raped and beaten by the security forces, so I didn't think justice would be served in Panama. That's why I launched on this high risk odyssey to get her out as a refugee. Please wish me luck. I'm only trying to do what I believe to be the right thing. You're usually an advocate for women. Surely you agree?"

He leaned and with his right hand gently caressed the back of her neck. She pushed his hand away, and they drove on in angry silence on the narrow highway and down into the Orosi Valley. "You are taking too many chances on everything!" she said with finality.

They headed across the valley for the Motel Del Rio, a beautiful tourist enclave, nestled under palms on the Orosi River. Lunch would be trout, freshly caught from a water-fall and stream nearby, with warm tortillas and beans. It would go well with a swim and a beer, Rob thought, though his pleasure was clouded by Sophie's anger.

The road they turned onto was rougher and somewhat winding. Sophie was becoming uncomfortable from the jostling ride.

"Let's pull over on that little track," she requested.

The track left the road and led down towards an orange grove. They got out onto the still wet grass as the morning sun continued its fiery ascent. So far, despite its intensity, it had missed burning the heavy wet dew off the lower lying banana plants and orange trees they pushed through. They were cooling on their skin. The sweet tangy scent of oranges was extraordinarily strong in the warming, softening air. They could hear whinnies and grunts; some kind of struggle was going on between horses they could not yet see.

Rob steadied Sophie's progress on the uneven ground. Hand in hand, they threaded their way through low branches hung with oranges, until they reached the rails of a small corral. A sweating and snorting chestnut stallion was heavily courting a smaller bay filly on the far side of the space. She trotted ahead, just out of range as he reached with outstretched neck and sniffed.

Their hooves churned up earth, grass and fallen oranges along the rails of the fence towards the corners where the stallion was nipping the filly's back and ears, snorting loudly. Suddenly, the stallion stood on his hind legs, and tried to mount her, biting her neck so she stood still and squealed as he plunged wildly. Horse sweat, pungent crushed oranges, and the hormones of coupling lay heavily on the moist air.

Sophie reached the fence first, with Rob very close behind her. She rested her forearms on the middle rail. He could feel Sophie's bottom pressing against the front of his trousers as he stood leaning over her, encircling her with his arms protectively, reaching for the upper rail.

She turned her flushed face and kissed him hard on the mouth. Then, breaking the kiss off suddenly, she mouthed, "Do me."

She turned back to watch the horses. Rob flipped her flimsy dress up over her hips and with his other hand, he undid his own trousers and slipped them down.

Sophie pushed her bottom out, leaning forward over the rail. Rob's hand brushed her loose dress up and pushed aside her wet panties. They moved together for a few minutes until Rob could hear her gasps and his own thundering heavenly rush came quickly after.

CHAPTER 11

Rob sat slouched in one of the two chairs facing the ambassador's desk, his arms crossed. Tired from the stress in Panama, he had not hurried out of bed this Monday morning. Sophie's protests and the warm glow of more love making had also kept him there. It was now midmorning. He tried to focus. In front of him, Ambassador Langman was standing behind his desk, speaking. Langman turned to look out the window over the panorama of rusting corrugated roof tops that was downtown San Jose.

"Ah, this other sodden Eden. Just look at the rain." He smiled ruefully, and dragged deeply from his cigarette. "Are you really paying attention?" then throwing back the last gulp of coffee from his cup, he turned. Rob jerked into a more erect position.

"Sorry we didn't get to see you Friday morning at the airport. Noriega bustled me off to the president. We had a chat and a very nice lunch. He put the case forward for a Security Council meeting to be held in Panama to examine the 'colonial' situation. He wants Canadian support in the General Assembly and in the Security Council, for a meeting to examine Panama's sovereignty over the Canal." Craig paused for a drag on his cigarette.

"I put it all in a telegram to Ottawa and copied it to our

UN ambassador in New York this morning."

Bending over the desk, he shuffled and searched the papers. "Here's a copy for you. It's an unusual request, but not one without precedent. Sometimes, the Council wants to get out to consult constituents, especially if they can head off trouble, meaning issues of peace and security."

"The Americans aren't going to be very happy, are they?" ventured Rob. "They've been treating the Panamanians very well with all sorts of revenue from canal traffic. They won't like this kind of challenge. It's a key American presence for control of the Western Hemisphere, isn't it? I mean, there are what, eighty thousand troops and who knows how many ships and planes down there at any one time?"

"Yes Rob, and you remember the Cuban Missile Crisis of a dozen years ago. The Soviets tried to place nuclear missiles bases in Cuba, barely a hundred miles off the US coast? It was as close as I ever want to see us get to nuclear war," he paused. "That, and Che Guevara tramping around in Bolivian and Peruvian jungles stirring up revolution. Doesn't give the US a lot of confidence in Cuban and Soviet intentions. I suppose the Soviets will back Panama's claims over the Canal to the hilt," Rob said.

"You bet. Anything to upset the US, which won't want any reduction in control over the Canal and its strategic base in Panama."

"I can't see there is much benefit for Canada in Panama backing the anti-colonial crusade, especially when it is led by General Torrijos, the corrupt strongman of the people, and his sidekick Noriega," questioned Rob.

"Yes, well, he would no doubt like to get his hands on more of the Colombian drug trade, and maybe even the presidency down the road. A fine pair to lead Panama into an independent and democratic future," Langman quipped, as he sat down with finality.

Rob looked up from reading, questioning, "After all that, you seem to say in this telegram that we should support the Panamanian initiative. What gives?"

"There's more than one way to skin a cat, Rob. By being supportive to both the Panamanians *and* the Americans, we can play the even handed fixer and come out ahead. It should bring Panamanian intentions out in the open and expose the risks as well. The Americans can always use their Security Council veto if things get too rowdy. I suppose the propaganda barrage will be hard to handle, but the US are experts at countering Soviet bullshit. In any case, I've forewarned the Americans of our likely intention to support the proposed meeting in Panama through their ambassador here.

"He didn't seem upset, though he wasn't too kind in his comments about the Panamanians, which I couldn't put explicitly in the telegram! So, when the time comes, I want you to go down to Panama to support our UN ambassador, if the meeting takes place. You can tell him what we've gleaned about the Panamanians from our recent relations with them..."

Langman paused, "It should be a good learning experience for you. It'll mean, though, that you'll have to clean up whatever mess you've created with your most recent consular case. And you know, I waited for you at the Hotel Panama Friday afternoon, but you didn't show, so I assumed you were otherwise occupied."

"That's an understatement," nodded Rob with a grimace. "Where do you want me to start? I was going to ask your advice at Tocumen airport, but didn't get the chance as you well know. Things really went off the rails. Middleton, the British consul, didn't want to keep Carmen Torres in the embassy any longer because she was not Canadian. Noriega's people were pressuring them to hand her over 'as the key witness' to what is now the 'Canadian murder.' So some Panamanian friends organized a van to help me evacuate her to Portobello, where we met some other friends with a sailboat and whisked her out in the middle of the night. They're right now sailing up to Cahuita, where I plan to pick her up later in the week."

"Wow," whistled Langman incredulously. "You sure stuck your neck out on that one. And your friends' necks too. She's not even a national. You don't know how involved she was in the murder, do you? God knows, I'm not very happy you took all those risks, with more to come. There could be serious diplomatic repercussions you know."

"Yes, but Noriega and his men are... I just couldn't do anything else but get her out of there, Craig. They would have killed her and called it justice served. Then whatever else was going on would have been swept under the rug, and we would be out of the way."

"Understood. But we'll have to go very carefully with the next phase. It's your ass on the line. I'll touch base with the British ambassador and Middleton to see what kind of repercussions there've been so far. I'll let you know. We may have to reassess your role in supporting the ambassador at the Security Council meeting if it does happen, but let's see how it goes. We're in a pretty good position with Noriega; he views us a friend in court – but we'll have a hard time getting him to conclude the Kevin Voth murder case if we are treating the prime suspect not as a fugitive from justice, but as a protected refugee. And maybe you've foiled his sovereignty plot!" Langman was almost shouting.

"We do have quite a bit of leverage though, considering the favor they have asked of Canada to support the Security Council meeting in Panama. But, in the end, I may have to hang you out to dry. So, as I said, tread carefully, young man."

Then almost as an afterthought he directed, "Oh, and number one, Rob, you better do up the consular reporting telegram with a copy to the Ministers office, also copied to the Central America desk and Consular Division, updating on Voth. Don't mention your prime suspect for now – details will come later. Let me see it before it goes out. Don't want to get us in more trouble with Ottawa at this stage."

Rob, smarting from his dressing down, knocked on Claude Sarasin's office doorframe on the way back down the hall to his own. Claude was the administrative officer who also did much of the consular leg work. He was a French-Canadian with a can-do attitude. Always cheerful – and always up for an adventure.

He first "discovered" Cahuita for the office. He had taken Sophie and Rob there for a wonderful weekend of walking on the long sandy beach studded with coconut palms, and snorkeling to gawk at the stunning schools of tropical fish swimming on the beautiful coral reef across the mouth of the bay. They had used the dugout canoe of a local fisherman, Old David, to get out to the reef. Rob shuddered, remembering their encounter with a fifteen foot shark that he had been assured by locals had never before appeared behind the reef.

They had gotten to Cahuita on the narrow gage railroad from San Jose through the rain forest to Limon, then south on the banana train through the plantations to Penshurst station. From there, it was in a dugout canoe to cross the river and on to Lam's Hotel in Cahuita in the back of an ancient dump truck. It was the only way to go.

"Hey, Claude!" Rob called airily, and Claude jerked his head up in surprise. "I had a few scrapes on this murder investigation in Panama. I got the prime suspect coming up the coast on a sailboat. She should arrive in Cahuita sometime Friday. I need your help to arrange a trip out there. Reservations at Lam's, and the use of David's dugout. Sound like fun? I want you to come. And did you get my fax with the refugee application? It should have come in from the British consulate Thursday night."

"*She*, huh? Yeah, pretty sketchy Rob. Not a lot to go on, with no documentation or anything. But let's see what she looks like before I give you a definitive answer," Claude grinned.

"Bastard. I'm sure she'll make the grade," Rob offered with a return chuckle. "And when you see her, I'm sure you won't mind helping her settle into San Jose for a few weeks, what with all your knowledge of low life and the nightclubs- it should be an easy job!"

"Yeah, sure. I sent a full application for her to Ottawa, so it's in the works. Sounds like my kind of assignment," Claude quipped. "I'll make sure to have a couple of bottles of Flor de Caña in my backpack – one for David and the other to toast our Friday night success when we land her."

"By the way, LACSA has a new flight from San Jose to Limon. Want me to book it for the way out? I guess you need to know, though the flight is new, the airplane is not. It's a vintage DC-4 left over from US transport command in the last war. Hasn't aged well, I understand. And the airstrip is on the beach, with a thatched-roof terminal that doesn't serve drinks!"

******

Carmen lay on some cushions on the foredeck, propped up on her elbows watching the shoreline sail into view. It was so peaceful on Gypsy Moon, with the prow gently cutting through the occasional white-topped blue wave and the expanse of the Caribbean before them. They had had fair winds since leaving Portobello four days earlier.

The image of Rob had not left her mind, except during the times when her anguish over losing Kevin had overwhelmed her and she'd cried. Sometimes, Belinda had held her, to comfort her. Mostly, it was just the warmth and kindness that they showed her that helped to reduce the sobbing.

She shifted her arm and looked around. Kevin, how she missed him. She had learned to love him so – his kindness, his cheerful persistence in teaching her English, especially when she tried so mischievously to slip back into Spanish when she was struggling for a word. What a brutal language English was... and nothing seemed to make sense!

He was so tentative, so shy when they were alone.

But he had wanted her to speak Spanish when they were making love.

She smiled when she remembered how things had developed. She had approached him for extra help, because she was feeling quite desperate at her lack of progress. It had taken some time for the private lessons at her flat to develop into more than language learning. He was so proud of his little family, his wife and children, his strong commitment, his religion. She found his attentions strange. At first, Carmen had avoided flirting and teasing, which she would have dearly loved in other circumstances. He was attractive, strong, blue-eyed – clear and assertive in his teaching. And he asked about her life, about her hard life, and how she had ended up in Panama.

It was Kevin who took the first steps that led to their intimacy. She had protested, but then had not resisted.

And then came the horrible day when her brothers had challenged him. She shuddered to remember them all leaving. Now she knew. Or maybe not. She couldn't believe they had murdered him. They were not as mired in tradition as all that. They were just not that kind of people.

Carmen's whole life was torn up, changing so suddenly. She was on her way to Costa Rica with strangers, and then who knew where? Fear and anxieties wracked her.

She raised her head and perched on her elbows. Rob again. She had known him for what, a week? He seemed so decisive, in control, protective, willing to take risks when there was virtually nothing in it except trouble for him. It had been such a short, brutal, and dramatic time, that she wondered if her feelings towards him were growing. Maybe it was just because she was so alone and the waters so deep.

Emotionally, she was drained. The rape had deadened her heart and the brutality of the two guards had numbed her soul. She had felt nothing during the escape from her flat, and during the time at the British Embassy, Carmen had was grateful for their kindness, but she had felt little but a dull throbbing.

That changed with the festival in Portobello – the music and dancing, the joyous reveling of people had rekindled the fire in her Latin soul. She smiled. The flame of her being was beginning to brighten. Still, she shouldn't have these thoughts of Rob...

"Carmen!"

She jerked.

"Better get below decks – we're approaching Bocas del Toro." It was Jim, leaning over her. Alarmed, she snapped out of her reverie and pushed up off her elbows as he continued, "We're heading into shore to get some supplies. And we need more diesel fuel. Better get into the hiding spot in the back cabin, in case we get searched."

Jim and Belinda had removed cushions and life preservers from under one of the births in the stateroom that Carmen occupied. It was cramped, and a bit musty, but smelled only of the sea. She had been in worse spots. And smuggling people was a serious charge, leaving aside that Carmen was a fugitive from Panamanian justice, whatever that was.

CHAPTER 12

The launch from the runway of El Coco International in LACSA's vintage DC-4 had been shocking, even by Rob's farm-based flying standards. His knuckles were white as he sat and grasped the arm rests of his seat.

"You didn't tell me when I agreed to this trip that the airplane had been exhumed from World War Two!" he growled at Claude, who only grinned from ear to ear.

"Yes I did! Hang on!"

As the pilots had started up the four engines one by one, they chugged into action after a brief period of rough running, except for the inboard engine on the starboard side, which had poured out black smoke. By the time warm-up was complete and they'd taxied to the runway for takeoff, it was coughing smoke fitfully.

Notwithstanding, Rob saw through the open cockpit door that the pilots hands were duly crossed on the throttles, which were pushed home, and all four engines wound up to deafening full power with the brakes still on, in precautionary takeoff mode. When it seemed the airframe could take no more, every bolt vibrating, the pilots released the brakes and thundered down the runway, staggering into the blue Costa Rican sky in short order. At altitude, when they throttled back and leveled out, the troubled engine immediately poured out black oil. Mercifully, the prop was feathered before it caught fire.

Rob shouted to be heard over the din, "Guess we'll be heading back! Have to take the train after all."

Claude grinned again in reply, shouting in Rob's ear, "Thought you were the barnstorming pilot who could take anything?"

But instead of turning back, they banked east for the short trip to the Caribbean coast, flying low enough over the dense rainforest that the startled faces of black and white monkeys stared up at the thundering bird in the sky.

The landing at the new Limon airport along the beach in the unwieldy aircraft was a feat of consummate piloting skill, particularly considering only three of the four engines were operating. Normally, airport runways are constructed perpendicular to sea fronts, so that the prevailing sea breeze in the day and the reverse land breeze at night assists pilots in their job of landing or takeoff, which are always accomplished facing into wind. The Limon runway had been hacked out of the low jungle swampland parallel to the beach, so that wind blew across the runway, morning or evening.

Rob swore softly to himself, then to Claude, "They're going to land in a stiff crosswind! Could be very exciting!"

As the pilot approached, right wing low, the whole airplane crabbed into the sea breeze in order to avoid drifting off course. The result was a last-minute swerving course correction just before touchdown, a hard thump onto the packed sand, and reversed propellers on the remaining three engines that threatened to shake loose every bolt and rivet in the aircraft.

After a hard swerve to the left, they jerked to a stop near the grass-roofed terminal. Rob and Claude, sweating profusely, unbuckled their seatbelts.

"Holy fuck," said a white-faced Claude, as they climbed down the stairs to kiss terra firma, shaking, but with grins of congratulations for the pilots, who were beaming.

"*Tengan cojones!*" (you've got balls!) Claude directed towards the pilots, not with total enthusiasm. He and Rob both looked forward to continuing their trip on the ground.

A narrow gauge train carried them south along the coast from Limon to Penshurst Station. The diesel engine with four cars chugged and teetered cautiously along the poorly aligned tracks through Bananita and several miles of coastal banana plantations. Rob and Claude sat happily on wooden benches in the open-windowed passenger car at the rear, shouting cautions at ragged black kids who ran alongside smiling and playing a hop-on game, oblivious to the dangers.

As they stepped down from the passenger car at Penshurst station, Rob rubbed his hips and back to recover from some of the jarring. They walked a hundred yards or so along a path to the river, where a large dugout canoe was held steady against the shore by two very black men who stood in the shallow water on either side of the boat.

"Whoa, all aboard for the cruise!" Rob needled.

"But you get the cabin with the ocean-view!" chortled Claude.

Under the guidance of the two assistants standing in the water, Rob and Claude climbed carefully over the gunwale as the boat rocked precipitously. They paid two *colones* to the black outboard operator in the rear, clad only in ragged shorts.

The journey was about to continue across the Rio Estrella for the final leg to Cahuita, when shouting from a ways down the path took their attention back to land. A large black woman, puffing from the strain and heat of hurrying down the path, struggled aboard at the last moment. She stood imperiously, glowering in the bow of the heavily laden boat for the mercifully brief journey across the river. Sporting a well-worn straw Panama hat and two very large woven grass carrying bags resting underfoot, she stared across the water as if to mesmerize it into tranquility.

After reversing offshore, the motor accelerated as the canoe lurched forward in a sharp turn upstream, causing the dugout to pitch precipitously and she nearly lost her perch, grabbing the gunwale wildly to stop herself tumbling into the drink. She then turned to scowl at the boatman in shorts operating the ancient outboard motor which was now spewing major volumes of smoke. He stifled a broad smile.

"Holy shit!" cursed Rob loud enough for only Claude to hear, as he gripped the side and they approached the far landing, where he could now see that the remainder of the journey to Lam's Hotel was apparently to be completed in the back of a large dump truck.

It was a vintage Dodge inherited from the US army, white star markings still visible on the sun-faded olive green. The driver stood at the rear tailgate, where two wooden cases were stacked and ready for them to use to clamber up. The driver reached for their bags as they approached, pitching them up unceremoniously towards the front of the dump box.

Claude headed first for the front of the box, where the end was higher, presumably to protect the cab. "Up here! We can hang on," shouted the grinning tour-guide, Claude.

It afforded waist-high grips to hang on for the apparently rough journey to come. Three other passengers and the lady with the straw bags stood swaying in the middle as they set off with a jerk, with a clutch that grabbed and smoked, and with very uncertain squealing brakes that ground menacingly against the bare steel of the brake drums whenever the driver slowed for the frequent humps. Miraculously, all stayed upright, most with a modicum of foot shuffling.

As they ground to a halt and jumped off the tailgate into the packed sand, travel bags in hand, Lam, a diminutive and sun-aged Chinese, greeted them at the door of his two-story sun bleached clapboard warehouse. A faded sign over the door proclaimed, Lam's Hotel. Its four upper rooms served as the only local hotel accommodation. Bags and boxes of supplies filled the space when clients were scarce.

They followed him through the open front double door into the office to sign the register, passing through a low doorway behind the ramshackle bar. Several tables completed the scene, and a small stage with black lights and a speaker system marked the only nightclub in the area. Lam offered in heavily Chinese accented Caribbean English, "No food tonight. Mama sick. Go down street. First I arrange. How about you go look at beach. Swim? Snorkel? Spearfish? Maybe you catch supper for tomorrow?"

A beautiful coral pink sunset arched overhead from somewhere in the west as the travellers started south down the white sand towards Punta Cahuita, beneath overhanging coco palms. The bay was breathtakingly beautiful.

Shinnying up and along one of the palms, Claude swung his machete deftly and three coconuts fell. Once down, he stuffed them into a string net bag along with the bottle of Flor de Cana rum and plastic straws brought from the bar.

As they walked much further down the beach, they could see David, who seemed to have no other name than "Old," sitting on a low stool beside his fishing shack. Six poles had been bludgeoned into the sand with a few random boards nailed on lower down. A torn tarp served as a roof, and a fishing net hung over one corner, almost dry. A wood-framed string bed occupied one corner.

"David, hello! It's Rob and Claude!" they hailed him from a distance.

David was a slight, emaciated figure, severely crippled in his shoulders and back from an accidental fall as a child. He had told them this on their first visit some months ago, in his halting Caribbean Spanglish. His dark wrinkled face lit up with a toothless grin of recognition as he caught view of them approaching in the dusk.

"*Benvenidos*, welcome," he shouted softly in return.

He was weather beaten, skinny and bent, but in no way pitiable. He stood and turned to greet them, running bony fingers through his curly gray hair and placing his other hand on the gunwale of a dugout canoe with pink and blue faded paint only just discernible on the bow, pulled up on the rocks beside the shack.

Claude bent down and unburdened his backpack, which by now was quite stuffed. The rum and green coconuts, a bag of rice and a bag of beans, salt, bananas, limes, and mangoes completed the picture that brought steady grins to David's weather beaten face, as they appeared.

Claude wielded his machete to hack the tops off the coconuts and deftly poured a shot of rum and squeezed a half lime into each. The three settled companionably against a nearby fallen palm on the beach, looking out to sea for any sign of the approaching fugitive sailboat.

"No sailboat this week," grunted David, whose one good eye was still sharp. "But something new last few weeks. Very fast powerboat come into bay, usually at night. Further up beach north of Cahuita, near Rio Estrella." He looked down and quaffed more of his drink. "Smugglers. I don't go near 'em."

On their return to the hotel, it was dark. As they approached, Lam stood from a creaky cane chair and motioned for them to accompany him down to Corina's place for their dinner. He lit a smoky kerosene hurricane lamp. As they shuffled down the dusty sand, not far from the hotel, a clapboard house on stilts with an extended roof that formed a veranda in front appeared out of the darkened night.

Two tables, illuminated by a single hanging light bulb, sat on the outside porch and Corina hurried out to seat them. Rob and Claude were introduced to the two other guests from the hotel, seated at the other table, who were also food refugees. One was a Latino in his early thirties, slim build, medium height, his black hair pulled straight back in a ponytail, sunglasses perched on his head. The other was heavier set, and Mexican, Rob guessed. They broke off their conversation for a nodded "*Buena sera*," then turned back to each other, huddled intently, virtually ignoring Rob and Claude.

Corina, dark curls bobbing and black eyes flashing, brought out the excellent dinner: crayfish stewed in coconut milk and spices, spooned onto rice and beans seasoned with cilantro accompanied by light chili fried green bananas. She set a cooling tamarind drink with lemon and sugar in front of them.

"Don't know if we should be drinking this," Claude wondered aloud. Rob raised his eyebrows questioningly at him. They would know by morning if it had been boiled or not.

"Scandalous," said Lam about the price Corina had asked for dinner – ten *colones* each, about a dollar fifty – when he came to pick them up. "But what can you do with the new tourist industry? And her son's no good, getting involved with these new foreigners hanging about," in an aside to Rob and Claude.

When they reached the hotel, he shook his head and pointed with his chin to the phone on the hotel bar when they finally stepped inside. "You call ambassador in San Jose for important message," he said.

When they had crossed the Rio Estrella earlier, Rob had seen the telephone line that swung low over the river to Penshurst Station and joined the railway's trunk line to Puerto Limon. When he picked up the receiver, the operator in Limon answered, and dialed the ambassador's home number for him.

Craig Langman was not a happy camper. "Very bad news, I'm afraid – your friends Jim and Belinda went into Bocas del Toro for diesel and supplies. Marine Guardia found your suspect. She's locked up, and Jim and Belinda have had their boat seized and are being charged with human trafficking."

Rob gasped, his face turning white.

"The local police allowed them one call to the Embassy here in San Jose. I think you better have a swim in the morning and head back here pronto. You better not try anything fancy– this is now a real consular case involving Canadians it seems. Congratulations on the next fuck-up!"

When Rob shared the bad news with Claude, he realized how much he anticipated seeing Carmen again. Now it was dashed and he was agonizing over leading Jim and Belinda into such danger. Even if they had been enthusiastic and selfless about it, he was now kicking himself for having gone ahead.

Claude tried to bolster his spirits. "From what I can see, you didn't have much option. They were the only way out. It was a matter of life and death. We just have to figure this new one out."

The two foreigners, now returned from Corina's, were sitting at a nearby table nursing their beers, and had fallen silent. They looked at Rob and Claude as Lam handed them two barely cool *cervesas*, *Imperial*. "Why don't you join us?" said the heavier set one in strongly Mexican accented English. It seemed they had overheard the gist of the conversation. "We have business connections in Bocas del Toro and regularly go back and forth. Maybe we can help."

"I need to hitch a ride down with you to get a friend of mine released from custody and get some other friends' boat freed, so they can sail back to the British Virgin Islands."

"Mmm, no. I can't take you down, but maybe we can

work something out down there. We have connections, you see." Pablo, who had introduced himself as a Columbiano, offered. Amado, the Mexican, said after conferring briefly with Pablo in Spanish, "We can help, but will need your passports to show to the authorities. And you might not get them back."

Rob groaned softly, his guts in a knot. From the sounds of it they were engaged in a clandestine business, and he shouldn't be making deals, especially in regards to so delicate a matter. Should he get in deeper?

Claude took him aside. "It's tough, but if they keep them, we could say they were stolen."

Rob wondered how they would get out of it – they would have to report them lost or stolen to the police and could do that back in San Jose. More important, however was the principal: could he bring himself to justify it? Especially if the scheme didn't work. He would certainly have to level with Ambassador Langman at some point.

What if these guys just ripped off their passports and something happened to Belinda and Jim? And what about Carmen? Could he trust them? It would mean putting his friends in the hands of probable drug runners. Yes, but now Jim and Belinda were in the hands of Panamanian security forces. Which was worse? And what if the connection between Carmen's escape and Kevin's murder came to light, if it already hadn't? So turning back to Amado and Pablo, Rob offered, hesitantly, "Yes, and we will be happy to pay you for the services when you get back."

"It seems your people may have some difficulty with the Panamanian authorities? Don't worry," smiled Amado, "we can fix that. And we will do it *por amor!*" And with a wider grin, he looked at Pablo and both raised their beer bottles in a conspiratorial salute. *"Salud! Amor! Dinero!"*

Two nights later, evening set in; dusk fell, then darkness. Rob adjusted his bottom to a more comfortable position on a chair of woven palm fronds as he sat nursing his second after dinner beer at Lam's, peering out the door into the chorus of cicadas in the gloom. He distractedly watched the geckos dart up and down the inside board walls catching insects.

When he had called the ambassador the day before to relate that someone with business connections might be able to help them, Langman had exploded. But they had stayed anyways for another night, even after the businessmen did not return the next day. Perhaps Sophie had been right. He should have come home immediately.

After two full days, he was now beginning to ponder the folly of trusting the "shifty foreigners," as Lam called them. But he hadn't really had a choice, had he? Of course, he could have returned to Puerto Limon to hire a boat —would that have worked out in Bocas del Toro? Would he have arrived in time to persuade the Panamanian authorities to release Carmen, and Jim and Belinda's boat? Dubious.

Or should he have abandoned them and gone back to San Jose as the ambassador had wanted, and worked through official channels? He had already taken major risks by trusting the unknown Pablo and Amado. And, from his experience, the official route would have been long, dangerous, and unpredictable. Particularly as the authorities were on the lookout for Carmen as a fugitive and he had now associated Jim and Belinda with her. What was it? In for a penny, in for a pound. Could be a lot more than that. He could lose all of them, and his job.

Claude was already upstairs, snoring the sleep of an untroubled conscience, when a figure appeared in the hotel doorway from the darkness beyond. Rob stood, unbelieving. She dropped her bag and surged across the floor to clasp him tightly as he rose from behind the café table.

"Rob, Rob," she managed through her sobs. "I thought I would never see you again."

He realized she was wet from the waist down as he held her. Carmen turned her face upward and they embraced, passionately for a long moment.

Lam suddenly appeared, from his office behind the bar, astounded. "Where you come from?" he demanded.

She briefly stared at Lam then looked back to Rob. They now sat on one chair, Carmen's arms around Rob's shoulders. Rob was confused, " My God, Carmen, you're here! Why in God's name did Jim and Belinda go into the port at Bocas del Toro anyway?"

"Something about needing more fuel because there was a storm threatening. He had to have fuel to keep Gypsy Moon pointed into wind if there was a serious blow-so we wouldn't capsize in the storm? I don't know? And the storm didn't come."

"Yeah, OK, that makes sense. So what happened in Bocas?"

"It was so awful. Dragged me off the boat. Locked me up. Questioned me. Said they had to call Panama City. I was so scared. Then this afternoon the Mexican, Amado, came into my cell. I thought he was a goon sent by *Seguridad* because the guards treated him like some kind of superior officer."

"Interesting," Rob surmised, "he obviously has some official status with the Panamanians."

Carmen went on, "He said I would have to trust him, and he showed me your passport. Said he would help me get to Costa Rica. There were a couple of guys with him who carried guns. I had no choice."

"Where were Jim and Belinda? Locked up too?"

"So then he got Jim and Belinda released. He told them outside at the dock, that he would tow their sailboat up the coast near Punta Mona into Costa Rican waters and cut them loose – they were to forget ever having seen Amado and his crew and his huge motor cruiser, and not to touch land until they were well to the north, to Islas del Maiz or San Andres. He said otherwise it would not go well for them."

"My God, they did it," Rob choked with excitement. "I don't know how but they did it. And you're safe." He wrapped her in his arms and gave her another hug, this time a long one. "And Jim and Belinda too."

"They blindfolded me and sat me on the rear deck," she went on. "Amado told me not to talk to anyone. But they were nice enough. Gave me a *cervesa* and some *empanadas* to eat. After they cut Jim and Belinda loose, it was some hours before they slowed again and turned to shore. They dropped me off in shallow water near the beach and told me to head for the lights. Here I am."

"And the passports?"

"Passports? They said nothing, and I never saw them after Bocas."

At this Lam broke his silence, staring meaningfully at

Rob. "Need food, shower? We have extra room upstairs. I show you. We talk in morning." And to Rob, he said in a low voice, "She very lucky. Guy is Colombian. Escobar. Drug runner. Could have thrown her off the boat because she knew too much."

Within half an hour, Rob was in bed, staring at the ceiling and pondering the miraculous events. He shifted naked on his single sheet because of the heat, with the light out. Moonlight shone through the windows at the front of Lam's hotel and over the flimsy partitions that divided the rooms. The floorboards creaked. Carmen appeared at the side of his bed, hair wet, wrapped in a towel.

"Your room is next door."

"Rob, I need you. I'm scared."

"Carmen, what are you doing here? You know we can't sleep together. It's unprofessional, and besides, I love my wife. Go and put your clothes on and we can lie here for a while."

"Oh, I get it. You don't like mestizo girls. I'm too black for you."

She dropped her towel, and Rob gasped at her beautiful, dark olive skin. Her small breasts and pert nipples. The beautiful curves of her hips.

"Oh God, how could you think that? You are so beautiful! But you don't owe me. It's what I do. And I didn't do it with the expectation that at the end of your journey to freedom you would pay me back in bed!" he stood.

"I understand, but how many times have you stepped in at great danger to yourself – and how you held me downstairs – do you think I could believe you don't care for me?"

She held him as they kissed. They slipped into bed and

kissed, deeply, passionately.

He protested, but she silenced his lips with hers and rolled on top. Carmen began to move, slowly.

CHAPTER 13

Rob touched his forehead as he headed down the rickety staircase. Miserable and guilty, he was jubilant underneath that the rescue had worked out. Then there was the matter of the passports to worry about. Carmen and Claude were already tucking into a breakfast of *gallo pinto con huevos.* He looked at the rice and beans with an egg on top. He could smell the excellent Costa Rican coffee.

"Buenos dias," Claude smirked sarcastically, "Hope you slept well!"

"OK, thanks." He ducked down and sat, somewhat awkwardly. "I see you two have met."

"Yes," nodded Claude, "and she's been telling me quite a tale."

Carmen averted her eyes from Rob's and concentrated on her breakfast, unusually shy. Claude's directness had upset her, but she was so relieved to be with Rob, she smiled openly. She had not stood to hold him as she desperately wanted to, or even to touch his hand. *"Buenos días. Usted parece bien,"* good morning, you seem well, she said formally instead.

"I guess the passports are the only problem," ventured Claude when Rob sat down barely acknowledging Carmen. "The others have been released and are on their way back."

"Yes. Thank God. For now we'll say they were stolen, which they were in a sense. At least they didn't give them back. Have we all packed?" replied Rob curtly.

Lam's ancient dump truck squealed to a halt in front. Shortly they rose to begin the journey back across the river, then onto the banana train from Penshurst station, and eventually from the coast at Limon, winding through the rainforest on the narrow gauge railway to San Jose on the four hour trip. They were pensive, subdued on the train, except for Claude, who chatted incessantly, and tried to get them to eat the boiled turtle eggs he bought from a vendor, for lunch.

It was fairly late in the afternoon by the time they reached the imposing Gran Hotel de Costa Rica on Avenida Central. Rob spoke with the reservations clerk behind a large mahogany desk and settled Carmen into a hotel room on the fourth floor. When the porter left, they kissed, long and deeply.

"This has to be the last time," Rob said finally, "and we have to forget about last night. It didn't happen."

Carmen turned, tears streaming, "I know, I know. But I can't. Just go!"

Saying he would see her in the morning, he went to his Embassy office in the Cronos Building to check for messages. On entering the secure area, he nearly collided with Craig Langman exiting his office.

"There he is, the wayward vice-consul! Good thing you aren't dead." The ambassador was not pleased that Rob had ignored his order to return immediately and was just showing up now, Monday afternoon. But he had been mollified somewhat by learning of the success of the mission from Claude.

"If you ever disobey me like that again, I'll see you're sent back to Ottawa," said Langman evenly, as duty required. "We've got a lot to talk about, but that will have to wait. The American ambassador, Chester Arnold, just called. Said he wants to see us right away. Says it's important to your safety. You better give Sophie a ring and tell her you'll be further delayed. We can talk in the car on the way over."

The American Embassy was an imposing neo-colonial style building in the suburb of Escaczu. It was a little piece of Massachusetts Avenue in the tropics, complete with columns flanking the entrance portico. A major colony of American ex-pats had grown up in the little town west of the center of San Jose.

The ambassador received them in his cavernous, flag-draped office. A Presidential seal adorned the wall behind his massive mahogany desk. Chester Arnold was red-faced and jowled, a bombastic Nixon appointee from the southern states. Nixon scowled from the wall. He was apologetic about the short notice and urgency for the meeting. They sat facing the ambassador.

"Craig, good to see you," he said. And, with a nod to Rob, "Welcome back son. You've been in some pretty dangerous territory. In fact, you may be lucky to be alive! Our mutual friend Lam has disappeared. Possibly gone for a swim with the sharks, or at least that's what my boys tell me. Thought you ought to know." Rob sucked in his breath.

"Guess he knew too much. He called our drug boys last night with the story of your daring escapade. You can kiss those passports goodbye, too, but at least we know about them, so they'll be hard to use. Didn't have much choice, I guess, according to Lam?"

Ambassador Langman was now staring hard at Rob. Incredulity and anger clouded his face on learning these details of his mission.

Arnold continued. "You may have to consider packing up and going back to Canada early. These are some very bad actors. You could be in danger, and your family could, too. But in the meantime, you could be of great use in the cause of justice."

Langman nodded and wiped his brow. Regaining his composure, he turned back to Ambassador Arnold.

"Well, Rob's been off on this rather complicated consular case in Panama," he glanced darkly in Rob's direction, "but tell us how we can be of help."

"Well, it looks like a fugitive financier, Robert Vesco, from Detroit has convinced President Figueres that he should be invited to settle in San Jose, where he has promised to make some major investments. Only problem is the two hundred million or so he plans to use has been raided from his partner Bernie Cornfeld's billion-dollar fund, Investment Overseas Syndicate, and our financial authorities are after him big time."

Langman whistled, "Shortcut to rapid development, so to speak."

"Yeah, but not for long," the American replied. "If we get our hands on him it will be a short project! He's signing up for four or five million, so we're confident his real mission is to invest in much more lucrative activities than long term development investment in Costa Rica."

Turning back to Rob, he said, "I understand his shady

Montréal bookkeeper, Paul LeBlanc, has moved in, four doors down from you. Keep an eye on him while you're still here. We think this guy Vesco is also going to get more involved in shipping drugs up through the Caribbean. He already has links to Noriega in Panama. You met one of them in Cahuita, name of Pablo Escobar!" He stopped and waited for a reply.

"Well, thank you," choked out Rob, not wanting to go into detail. "We'll sure keep our eyes open. I don't want to get Sophie too involved, though; she's in an advanced state of pregnancy and is feeling pretty vulnerable."

"Well that's understandable, son. Don't you go taking any chances with the little woman. The drug runners may be planning a trip to San Jose to meet with Vesco. I'd hate for you to run into them. Here's a card with a number you can call to report anything or to ask for armed security assistance anytime of the day or night."

Rob began to protest but Ambassador Arnold ducked his head and waved to cut him off, "I know you Canadians don't have such resources at your disposal. And don't hesitate if these bad dudes seem to notice you or try to contact you in some way. You could be in serious danger. The Costa Ricans have zero capability to help. They wouldn't have a clue what you are talking about and would deny it if they did.

"What about this little Latina girl you rescued? Where did you leave her? We can't go near her to try and debrief her – it would be a certain death sentence. We don't know much about her, but it seems rather strange those drug runners would treat her so well."

Rob protested, "Well, *Seguridad* raped her and beat her

to get her to confess to the murder of the missing Canadian school teacher, Kevin Voth. I don't believe she could have been involved."

Arnold interjected, "Isn't it surprising though, that they were able to get her out of Panama so easily, the way they are connected. We speculate that either she was in cahoots before, or they were able to recruit her on their motor boat. It's all a bit fishy. You need to get her somewhere safe fast, where she can be questioned and then be under surveillance."

Rob thought better of replying at this point. Hadn't Carmen told him clearly of her fears? And that she was confused by the kind way that she had been treated onboard the boat? And she had been delivered safe. But why? Were they just being honorable, or would they recruit her for some return down the line? Swirling questions with no answers.

But could he level with her without compromise? His heart said yes, but his thoughts wandered back to her two brothers. Why hadn't they been around to look after her welfare? They'd just vaporized. And Carmen had not told him anything. He would have to be careful.

CHAPTER 14

Rob arrived home just at dinnertime. He reached for the door and unlocked it. Sophie burst on him as he came through the door. Her face was flushed with anger. He blinked. She was even more beautiful than before. And very pregnant. Through her tears of rage and distress she cried,

"How could you not be here? You have no idea of the horrible time I've been through. And they couldn't get you in Cahuita last night – the line was down to Lam's Hotel. I was so worried!"

"You, you know I love you, sweetheart," Rob stammered as he tried to embrace her. "Tell me what happened!" She avoided him and pulled away, fists up.

"Where have you been, and how is it that you couldn't even call me again? All alone. You know what state I'm in."

"I'm really sorry," Rob whispered hoarsely in her ear as they finally clung together, Sophie like some unstable fishing float bobbing on the sea, sobbing uncontrollably. She continued,

"Last night the cat was in heat and climbed up on the garden wall, howling like a lioness. Just before midnight, Senior Keith from next door, drunk as a lord, pounded on the door. He took the opportunity to leer and slaver while berating me not being able to sleep because of the cat's racket. It took me ages to talk him out of a further scotch, which he demanded for his trouble. And then I had to go out in the back garden and stand on a chair to retrieve that wretched Siamese. I fell getting off the chair with Taja in my arms. I've felt rather strange ever since," Sophie sobbed. "I think the baby is coming, Rob. I've felt some contractions."

They began in earnest at about three o'clock in the morning. By seven, when the contractions were five minutes apart, Rob phoned Clinica Santa Rita to alert them they would be coming for the delivery.

Sophie had arranged for him to be present at the birth. He was in fact an important part of the process. Dressed in surgical gown, he stood at bedside clutching her perspiring hand and encouraging her, as the contractions increased in intensity and frequency and her breathing became deeper and faster to try to stave off the pain.

Rob's mind flashed back to when they had first met in the Rockies. How beautiful and wild and vulnerable and young she had seemed. Like a tiger kitten, with her lithe body, her determined and quick mind, and her vivacious personality. He had been smitten. During the first years of their marriage, he had been very anxious, crushed by her early unfaithfulness with a very attractive young lawyer.

She was exploring what else there might be out there. When she came back, they reconciled. But his confidence had been shattered and he frequently felt he would never be enough for her, that Sophie would always be looking for something more than he could give her. She came from a wealthy and powerful family, and he had always felt like his upbringing on the farm was just another proof of his inadequacy.

As he looked down on Sophie's beautiful face, contorted with pain as it was, he felt a chaotic mixture of emotions. Love, because she had wanted his child, and guilt for not being there for her in her need the previous evening. But he now had the opportunity for redemption. He was at her side for this most critical time.

"Push! Push! The baby is coming!" the nurse yelled, "Doctor Salazar! *Venga!*"

Rushing to the foot of the bed, he watched transfixed, as the doctor held the baby's head and urged her to come out the last few difficult moments. He turned to Rob with the baby in his hands.

"Hold her!" he commanded brusquely as he turned to cut the cord. She cried out briefly. Rob looked at her. The moment became metaphysical and surreal; there was a new tiny being cradled in his arms. Then they laid her on Sophie's breast. There was no adequate explanation of his feelings at the arrival of this new living, breathing, being, in Sophie's and his image.

The next few days blurred in a nightmare chain of nursing, changing, meal preparation, car rides, and walks. Rob wondered how he could survive on so little sleep. And he had forgotten all about the conversation with the American ambassador until he saw the LeBlanc kid riding by on his bike. Or at least he assumed it was the LeBlanc kid: there was a Québec flag flapping jauntily from the handlebars. With the baby coming and all his preoccupations, Rob had not told Sophie about the conclusion of his Cahuita venture, or about the conversation with

Chester Arnold.

Sophie was shocked and frightened by the news, realizing how vulnerable they were to danger. She was not at all keen on the American ambassador's proposal to keep an eye on the LeBlancs. Rob agreed that the best strategy was to keep a low profile. Ambassador Arnold's suggestion that they consider leaving the post early hit hard now that they were surfacing from the flood of new baby preoccupation. He didn't even think of Carmen until he returned to the office.

CHAPTER 15

Rob pushed the elevator button for the sixth floor. As walked across the lobby, Marielos tossed him a cheerful *com'estas la bambina,* from behind the reception desk. It had been nearly a week since he last set foot in the office. He bent and air-kissed her on both cheeks, telling her how well things were going with little Julia and her mom. He pushed the code buttons on the security door handle. Once, then again. Off his game.

Rob started down the hall and paused when he got to Claude's door. He turned in suddenly without knocking. Claude looked up, startled.

"She's gone. Carmen's gone. Checked out," Claude said evenly, "two days ago. She left you this note." He pushed it across the desk. Rob, shocked, picked it up. He read from the Spanish:

Dear Rob,

My brothers' friend is taking me to Guatemala. He says I'm not safe here and must go. Pedro and Hernan are alive but are being held by Seguridad under charges of killing Kevin. He says there is a Canadian office in Guatemala City where I can go for my refugee status. I do not know how I will get there or what will happen but I will try. Please send them a message to look out for me. I hope I will see you in

Canada. Vaya con Dios.

Muchísimas gracias y amor, Carmen.

He sat heavily, elbows on his knees, head in hands. "My God I'm too late."

"Nothing you can do. She was gone when I went to the hotel Monday morning. I tried getting the Costa Rican *Guardia Rurale* to watch for her at the border. No word back."

"Have you sent anything to the consular office in Guatemala City to look out for her?"

"Yes, I did that right away. I also faxed them a copy of the refugee form that I sent to Ottawa earlier, so there's not much else to do." Claude offered with finality.

"And Middleton called for you from Panama. When I told him you were at home with the birth of your new baby, he said he needed to speak with the ambassador. Maybe you should call him before you talk with Langman."

Rob hadn't anticipated how quickly things seem to be falling apart. After a couple of harrumphs, Middleton began slowly, "...very gruesome news. Bad, I'm afraid. Severed head sent us in a postal bag...the taxista, Johnny. With a bullet hole in his forehead. Presumably shot with my Wembley which was returned in the same bag."

"Oh my God. I am so sorry. At least we got Carmen out. But she's gone from the hotel where we put her up. Did Claude tell you?"

"No. But let me finish," Middleton continued testily, not pleased with the interruption, "one of our local staff was able to find Derek – wouldn't come to collect the remains – too dangerous. Said Johnny told him he'd been under pressure from *Seguridad* ever since he picked you up at the airport that first day. In fact someone called Captain Rios apparently directed him to take you to Kevin Voth's body in the canal zone."

"So it wasn't Johnny's sixth sense that led us to the discovery. Thinking back, it all makes sense now. He was working for *Seguridad* all along."

"I don't think we can assume that. Probably just the usual pressure at the beginning. At least he went rogue after he saw how badly Carmen had been treated. He risked a lot, obviously, to line up Derek and help you with the escape plan. I don't know when *Seguridad* figured it out, but I can only imagine that he would've been tortured badly to get all the details before they killed him. The wrath of Noriega. And they didn't want him leaking to you the full extent of the plot."

"You mean to enable us to figure out the possible sovereignty angles?"

"Yes, I suppose so. Those were largely kiboshed by their inability to pin the murder on an American anyway. Your taking away their principal witness has undermined plans too."

"Does it look like he fingered Derek?"

"Perhaps not, but he wants to lie low. We'll be leaving Johnny's remains with a priest at San Isidro on Derek's instructions. Family members will pick them up there and give him a burial. Lord knows where the rest of him is. So it looks as if we will be suspending further investigation into Voth's murder. Our hands seem to be tied for the present!"

"So sad. So brutal. I guess you did warn me, things could get lumpy, " Rob smiled ruefully at his own naivety, "any news on Carmen's brothers, Pedro and Hernan? Carmen left a note saying they were in custody and had been charged with Kevin Voth's murder."

"Really? That's news to me. I wouldn't recommend you come down to follow up. We'll try and make some discreet inquiries after things settle down."

"Thanks. I'll be going down the hall in a minute to find out what my fate is from the ambassador. So thanks very much Jack for all your help. We'll be in touch."

He rose and walked slowly down the hall towards the corner office. Portraits of Queen Elizabeth and Prince Philip lined the walls along with a rogues gallery of Langman's predecessors. The door was closed. Donalda, his executive secretary looked up.

"Just knock and go in. He's expecting you."

Craig Langman's stern face broke into a smile as he came around from behind his massive desk, hand extended.

"Congratulations Rob on your new little girl. How's Sophie bearing up?" He was overly upbeat.

"She's fine really. Little Julia is nursing well. But Sophie's been very anxious since I shared the American ambassador's comments about Vesco, LeBlanc and the drug runners coming to town."

" Yes, well, Middleton's report on the gruesome fate of your taxi driver has really put a lid on it for me. I've recommended to Ottawa your family's immediate recall."

"You mean right away?" choked Rob.

"Yes. I've decided not to let things develop here. Sorry you won't be able to be here but best you and your family go back to Ottawa. I don't think it's safe for you to go down to Panama to brief the UN ambassador for the Security Council meeting. I'll handle that.

I know it's a disappointment, but it's the best course in the circumstances."

"So you think I should have handled it differently and now you're sending me home?"

"No Rob, it's not like that. Your strong sense of justice lead you down the path you took – to do what you did. I would probably have done much the same at your age. There is no right and wrong to this, only choices. You made choices that now put you and your family at serious the risk. There's nothing much more you can do now, so I'm making the choice for you to go home. You've got a great future. Get on with it."

PART TWO

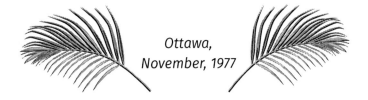

Ottawa,
November, 1977

CHAPTER 16

Rob stroked the stubble on his chin. It was near the end of the afternoon, as he turned to look through his tall office window overlooking the National War Memorial. He always felt a thrill coming to work so near the centre of power. Parliament was just across Wellington Street, and the Prime Minister's and Cabinet offices were just around the corner.

His thoughts wandered to Sophie and their abrupt return to the nation's capital more than three years before. Now Rob felt a surge of anxiety about that whole episode in his life: a US intelligence assessment had just come across his desk tying Noriega, Robert Vesco, and the Caribbean drug trade to Halifax and Montréal, rekindling memories.

He had not thought often of Carmen since she had fled to Guatemala just before his and Sophie's hasty departure from Costa Rica. Some time ago he had learned that her refugee status had been processed and she had finally made it to Canada. From there, the trail had gone cold. Carmen had made no attempt to contact him. And he had not tried to find her.

Three years of political assignments in Foreign Affairs had intervened since returning from Central America; a year in public affairs as a flak, handling NATO and

European Community issues, and then two years in Eastern European division. It was there that he had learned to manage the counter-intelligence activities that seemed to overlay all aspects of relations with Eastern Europe. So he had been Personnel's natural pick for his recent assignment as Coordinator of Intelligence in the Cabinet Office. But he was finding the flow of documents and information from the five Canadian agencies involved in counterintelligence and international liaison with the "five eyes" intelligence partners somewhat overwhelming.

Rob touched his forehead, recalling that he had first learned of the links and sharing of tasks in the wider intelligence community years before, during his initial assignment in the Special Research Bureau that dealt with strategic economic issues like oil supply or the state of the Soviet grain crop. The US, Britain, Australia, and New Zealand had forged this close, officially linked intelligence community during the war, gathering and sharing intelligence from a multitude of sources on threats and challenges from around the world.

Canada's largest ongoing contribution to all of these efforts was in defensive counter-intelligence, mainly in the vast northern wilderness, where hi-tech, over-the-horizon radar and electronic eavesdropping monitored Soviet military preparedness to attack the US and Canada over the pole with manned bombers and intercontinental ballistic missiles. It also involved a major role in North Atlantic nuclear submarine detection, surveillance, and air and naval interdiction. The North American Air Defense System, NORAD, tied the joint command structures together.

In exchange, Canada received many reports and assessments on issues and threats gathered from partners' operations in the rest of the world. He marvelled at his own role in this reality and the almost collective numbness and fatalism in the face of the unthinkable: the overwhelming threat of massive mutual nuclear destruction if the balance became unstuck. Constant vigilance, preparedness and balance were the main requirements of preventing this Cold War from heating up.

This wide community of intelligence meant incredible volumes of information flowed into Canada – to and through five agencies: Foreign Affairs, the Communications Security Establishment, National Defense, the Solicitor General, and the RCMP Security Service. Assessments and briefings compiling the highlights of this information gathering flowed from these agencies to the Cabinet Office.

It was at times a gargantuan effort that Rob and the Secretary to Cabinet for Intelligence and Security faced daily, along with Colonel John Gregory from Defense. Their Joint Intelligence Committee reviewed the reports and assessments that they prioritized, and then Rob edited and summarized them and put them forward through the Secretary for the Cabinet's use.

It had been dark for more than an hour when Rob began clearing up his top secret files, putting them in his in-tray and locking them away in his safe.

Sophie had gone to the west coast for ten days with little Julia, ostensibly for a rest and to recharge her batteries with her recently retired parents on one of the Gulf Islands. He smiled as thoughts of them unwound his tension. Sophie was happy, he thought, though it had not been easy settling back into Ottawa. At least she was pursuing her own career at the university, though always paying close attention to their daughter's needs. Was he sharing enough of the load?

Sophie was restless still, he knew. Rob had turned a blind eye to her explorations with other men – he felt unsettled that she might leave - he loved her and their little daughter.

He locked up and headed for a restaurant in the Byward market – it would be dark and cold and lonely when he finally got home tonight.

Brightly colored lights that shone through the windows and the cheerful beat of the Latin music that poured from Las Palmas lifted Rob's gloomy mood. He pushed through the door and hovered near the empty reception desk, waiting for the hostess to return. Scanning through the rough wooden tables, the potted palms and the color-ful rustic Mexican village murals painted on the walls, nostalgia surged for his time in Latin America. When she returned, he felt good about asking the South American hostess in Spanish for a table near the stage, where he could get a better look at the three beautiful Latinas belting out a Colombian folk song.

As he moved to his table and prepared to sit, he looked up. The beautiful singer in the middle, rubbed the ratchets on a gourd with a drumstick, her beautifully rounded hips and thighs flowing with the merengue beat. She smiled as she belted out the throaty tune, and then her voice caught as their eyes met. It was Carmen.

She ended the song quickly and hurried to his table. Rob stood and embraced her, dumbstruck. They kissed. After a few moments they sat breathless, staring at each other. People at other tables turned and stared, then laughed and clapped.

"My God…," she was struggling. "How long has it been?"

Rob ordered a couple of Coronas and looked at her questioningly.

"I spent a few years in Montréal, and I've just moved to Ottawa with my friends to start this folklore group," she began.

"Why didn't you contact me? You could've at least let me know you were alive." His anger flashed.

"You know," she said hesitantly, "it's a long story. After I arrived, my brothers showed up. They told me not to be in touch with you. They've been in Montréal off and on doing business. And besides, I wasn't sure you'd want to see me again. Can we go home after the show and I'll cook you something decent and we can talk?"

"You mean they're not in jail in Panama?"

"*Pues*, no," Carmen said deliberately, she looked down. "They were for a while, but their sentences were very short. Anyways, I'll tell you more about it later. Let's go after the next set."

As Carmen rose to return to the stage, Rob's hand stopped her, and he said darkly, "Of course, we have a lot to talk about."

The Blue Line taxi deposited them at a white clapboard two-story house on Fifth Avenue in the Glebe – it was fast becoming a trendy area for government people on the way up. Carmen was still flushed as she unlocked the darkened front door and led him by the hand into the front hall, very proud of her new house. Rob looked around as the lights came on. It was quite run down and needed a lot of work, but cheerful Latin American art was everywhere, and it was cozy. Renovations were in progress in the basement stairwell, so boards were piled in the hall and sawdust abounded. It was roomy and reasonably well furnished with older, unmatched pieces.

"Friends from Montréal helped me get it!" She gushed. "Not bad for a poor refugee, *eh*?"

"Looks wonderful," offered Rob. "Pretty big for one person..."

"I'll have to take in boarders to make ends meet. Another friend is fixing up the basement for someone to stay in," Carmen said as she pulled a large plate piled with pupusas out of the fridge and put a frying pan on the stove. "Would you like some wine while you wait for these to heat up?" He nodded.

"Here. Can you open this?" Carmen handed him a corkscrew. She watched him react with surprise to the French label on the bottle of wine she placed on the table.

"Yeah," she said smiling, "from the Colombian ambassador. My day job is at the Embassy."

The dinner was small talk about settling into Ottawa and reminiscing about Cahuita and Panama. Rob told her about the gruesome fate of Johnny and his ambassador's direction not to return to Panama. Carmen was appalled, then didn't reply directly as Rob continued to probe about her time in Montréal and the whereabouts of her two brothers.

"Oh, they've been up here a couple of times over the last year or so. They're doing some business; I don't know what, exactly." Carmen rested her elbows on the table, her hands steepled, holding a glass of wine. She looked over it into Rob's eyes.

"They travel in the Caribbean, but they don't talk about it. They just stay with me for a few days and we have a good time...let's go into the living room," she said, and rose from the table.

Rob followed her, eyes riveted on the sway of her hips, and set his wine on a low table. She turned and smiled. He looked into her deep brown eyes as she tossed her luxuriant, kinky reddish hair. He ran his fingers through it as he pulled her close. Her musky warm scent was strong. Rob couldn't resist taking her in his arms and cradling her breasts against his chest. Her tight pants firmly pressed his hips. He kissed her deeply; her mouth was eager.

"Aah... You like me!" Carmen murmured huskily. "Come on upstairs, where we'll be more comfortable." She led the way. They undressed and moved together, kissing and stroking. She turned back the sheets. Rob was in a love trance: everything he did, Carmen responded to eagerly. Their lovemaking was passionate, deep and flawless – sharing the ecstatic moments with neither leading nor doing anything that had to be calculated.

After an endless dream-like night of making love, interspersed with gentle sleep, their bodies spooning together, Rob awoke early, refreshed. Carmen still slept, breathing softly on the bed. The beauty of her hair spread across the pillow, her parted lips, the curve of her breasts and hips, and the luxuriant down between her legs held him.

Yet he was riven by confusion. She had not been willing to tell him much about Pedro and Hernan- still the principal suspects in Kevin Voth's murder to his mind. What was she hiding? He hurriedly pulled on his strewn clothes and headed down the stairs before dawn. He would walk in the morning chill to his home nearby on the Rideau Canal to shower and change and get to work by eight o'clock. He would see if Sophie had left any anxious messages.

Rob halted at the front door, as naked Carmen spoke softly from the top of the stairs. "You didn't kiss me goodbye. Will I see you again?"

Rob turned and smiled, and for an answer came to the top of the stairs and kissed her, holding her warm nakedness close.

CHAPTER 17

Colonel John Gregory turned from where he sat in front of Rob's desk, peering at a morning newspaper, coffee mug in hand.

"Hard night-shift at the factory?" he asked, tilting his head to one side and checking his watch as Rob rushed breathless through the door. It was 8:05 a.m.

Rob had a lot of time for Gregory, who was good humored, crisp, and to the point. He was a recent convert to military intelligence, and was now assigned to the cabinet office after a long tour in peacekeeping in Egypt and Cyprus. Semi-retirement, he called his new job. He hadn't yet gained the arrogance and cynicism often prevalent in seasoned intelligence hands.

Rob hung up his coat on the rack behind the desk and took his chair, smiling. "Yes, tough night all around. Heavy production is why I'm so much behind schedule," he grinned. "And to what do I owe the pleasure of this early-morning attention?" he asked. Normally, everyone sat alone at their desk for the first hour, scanning newspapers, checking out new overnight reports, and setting the day's priorities.

"We've got an emergency situation coming on with a Soviet nuclear powered spy satellite. Its elliptical orbit over North America is decaying and becoming critical, below a hundred miles. It'll soon re-enter the atmosphere and either burn up or crash."

"And if it crashes, is there fallout?" Rob raised his eyebrows. "Have the minister responsible for public security and the prime minister been alerted?"

"That's what I'm here about," offered Gregory. "The defense minister has the news through NORAD, and so does public security. We need to get a report up to cabinet and the PM, fast. The complication is that we obviously need to warn the public about the dangers, without causing widespread panic. But the other, more pressing issue is how to manage our US friends who won't let us: they don't want to reveal how well NORAD systems can track satellites, nor that we have their specifications in such detail."

Rob shifted uncomfortably in his chair. "Well, what's the real risk of the decaying satellite plowing into a populated area with its nuclear payload? There is an awful lot more snow and tundra than people up here. Do we have detailed information on where it's likely to hit the ground?"

"That's just the problem. It's tumbling. The Americans don't know exactly how soon the decay of the orbit will bring it down, and they don't know if it will burn up in the atmosphere, or if the nuclear reactor can withstand the heat of re-entry and actually hit the ground intact and then maybe blow up, or even where Cosmos 954 will hit the ground. It could be in the sea, a US city, or here. A lot depends on its speed of re-entry."

"That's a cool name, Cosmos 954. Too bad it's linked with a possible major disaster," Rob smiled.

Gregory frowned and placed a piece of paper in front of him.

"Top Secret. Draft memo to Cabinet. Just the facts. Have a look and make changes. We'll take it in to the deputy secretary before he chairs the JIC at ten o'clock. It could be up in time for the Cabinet meeting at eleven this morning."

"Looks good," Rob said a few moments later. "Only thing I would suggest is a revision to the public communications strategy. We have to do more than this. Let's talk to the DS. Maybe we can make reference to some public observatory breaking the news on Cosmos. We'll find a way to obfuscate the sources. Then we'll have to warn the Americans what we are going to say."

Rob was exhausted by the time he headed down through security to the Sparks Street Mall for a late lunch. The morning's struggle with defence intelligence on protecting sources and holding the line on a public announcement had been very stressful, considering what was at stake. Finally a compromise was reached, in which an anodyne version would be run past intelligence liaison in the US Embassy before the announcement. Someone from Foreign Affairs would walk it over right away, because time was very short, and lives could be lost.

But despite all that, he burned to see Carmen, the passion of the previous night flooding his mind. He couldn't use his office phone because he knew it was closely monitored. God, what was he turning into, he wondered, as he slid his quarter into a payphone. There was no answer at home, so he left a message to meet him at Las Palmas after work if she could. Guilt filled his mind as he tucked into his spaghetti bolognaise and mixed green salad. A glass of red wine. He must be crazy to be thinking like this.

The afternoon debrief in the deputy secretary's office on the weekly intelligence report he had delivered to Cabinet dragged. Rob exchanged glances with Ted Czernak, who rose to outline the solicitor general's departmental view on the drug trafficking report from the Americans that had triggered Rob's reverie about Panama. His doubts about Carmen and her brothers suddenly came into focus.

When the man sat down, Rob leaned over and asked in a low voice, "Could you check something out, Ted? A few years ago I ran into a couple of brothers in Panama on a consular case that have shown up in Montréal. Maybe drug related. Just a hunch, but I wonder if you might check them out. I'll give you a short note."

Rob had mixed feelings as he walked the last two blocks down past the old market parking garage towards Las Palmas, hands thrust deeply into the pockets of his open overcoat. As he stepped off the curb to cross Murray Street to the restaurant, a sharp whistle came from somewhere down the street. Carmen grinned mischievously from the open driver's window of her clapped out little red Honda Civic.

"*Aqui!* Down here," she shouted. He paused, spotted her waving hand and headed over.

As she drove, they argued volubly about why Carmen had not tried to contact Rob from Montreal during her three years there. As the car sped towards her house in the Glebe, she seemed nervous and somewhat anxious, glancing sideways at Rob from time to time, so he became nervous she would run into something.

"Hey, watch where you're going," he finally shouted at a near miss going through a red light. "Want me to drive?"

"Rob, we're going home because I have to meet someone from Montreal. He probably wants me to go back for the weekend."

"What's going to happen? Are you going?" demanded Rob, not at all pleased with the arrival of a likely Montréal boyfriend.

They were just inside Carmen's house, and she was bending to open the living room blinds, as a black Audi Coupé with tinted windows pulled up. A muscular man of medium height bounded up the stairs in his sharkskin suit and mirrored aviator glasses. He clasped Carmen tightly as she greeted him at the door and air-kissed her three times on her cheeks, as she avoided his lips.

"It's good to see you," Carmen said with evident delight. "What brings you to Ottawa?"

"What do you mean?" He pushed her away as he growled in heavily Haitian-accented English, "I thought you would be ready to go!"

"Oh, you mean it's time for Pedro and Hernan's monthly visit. I'm kind of busy so I thought I would skip it this weekend. I'm supposed to be performing at Las Palmas tomorrow night," she said, glancing over her shoulder somewhat furtively. "Here, come and meet Rob! Rob this is Emanuel Jean."

"Enchantez, je suis sure," he said dismissively between clenched teeth, pointedly not extending his hand. "You know, Carmen, they're asking to see you particularly. So let's go."

"Why don't you sit here in the living room and make

friends? I'll go and get you both a beer and pack a bag. Then we can go."

Carmen returned with two beers and set them on the coffee table between them without glancing at Rob. She focused on Emanuel and smiled at him. "I'll be down in a minute," she said, turning and hurrying up the stairs. A moment later, she called, "Rob, can you come up here and bring that bag I left in the hall?"

Rob picked up some shopping she had left near the front door and vaulted up the stairs two at a time. Carmen pulled him into her bedroom and shut the door.

"Careful, Rob, you understand... I have to go."

Rob hissed, his heart in his mouth, " What's going on? Will you be safe? Is he your lover?"

"From another time, another place," Carmen winced, "and you can't believe how much I don't want this to be happening here and now. But I have to go."

"Then I'm coming too," Rob said impulsively.

She looked at him pleadingly, "That's impossible. It can't happen."

"Then I won't let you go!"

"I have to. Okay. Come and meet me tomorrow noon in Place Jacques Cartier, in Old Montréal. There's a little restaurant just off it called Le Jardin. If I'm not alone, you'll have to pretend you don't know me. If that doesn't work, then at Notre Dame Cathedral just before mass at six. Now you have to go. Here, I'll give you Marie-Sol's number in Montréal. She's the only one who'll know where I am."

Rob hurried down the stairs out onto Fifth Avenue and down to the corner of Bank Street to hail a cab. At his empty home on the other side of the canal, he found Ted

Czernak's number and called him. Ted had received no reports back from Montréal on the brothers, but readily agreed to meet Rob at the Solicitor General's offices at nine o'clock on Saturday morning. He had some news.

CHAPTER 18

Rob was on the road to Montréal just before ten. At a steady seventy miles per hour, he planned to hit Old Montréal shortly after noon, just in time to meet Carmen at Place Jacques Cartier. Ted Czernak's contacts with police intelligence had turned up nothing on the two brothers, but they expected biker-gang drug activity over the weekend, with rumors of a large shipment of cocaine arriving in Montréal via Halifax and the Caribbean. Ted had given him numbers for two inspectors in the Montreal and RCMP drug squads that he had alerted, should Rob need them. But he had cautioned him to stay clear. This is not your game, he had said.

The weather was cold and bright with some snow on the ground, but there was little wind and no threat of a storm. The road was clear and Rob kept up a steady pace until he took the Bleury Street exit to Old Montréal. He drove a short distance down Boulevard Notre Dame in heavy traffic and turned into a small parking lot halfway between the Basilica Notre Dame and Place Jacques Cartier.

As he strode down the street towards the waterfront, dominated at his back by the enormous grey stone Hotel de ville, he was confronted by a fire eater and other noisy buskers, including Bonhomme Carnaval, already advertising Winter Carnival in Quebec City. They had attracted a few hardy souls surrounding them in straggling circles in the snow. Rob managed to duck around and continued to the end of the square turning left into a small side street, where he spotted Le Jardin.

Warm air and the smell of good food flooded out as Rob pulled open the door to the restaurant. He locked eyes with Carmen standing a short distance away. Alarmed by his sudden appearance, she turned away quickly, smiling at and cajoling the two Latino men in open parkas in front of her, who were stamping their feet and complaining bitterly in Spanish about the frigid weather. They stood in a longish line, waiting to be seated. Rob cursed his luck and turned quickly to back out, bumping into patrons pressing in behind him.

He crossed the street to a small place that had no lineup and took a table near the window with a view of the Le Jardin door from across the street. He ordered a Croque Monsieur with a beer and sat back to wait for Carmen to appear. He caught a glimpse of her, through the fogged window, hands describing 'who knows what' in earnest conversation with the two men.

Were they her brothers? Had they or had they not killed Kevin Voth? How much was Carmen not telling him about her involvement? After a futile hour of agonizing about the whole situation, they were still sitting and waving their arms, so he left.

Just before six o'clock Rob joined the throng streaming into the ornate Basilica Notre Dame for mass, a few blocks down the street from Place Jacques Cartier. His eyes quickly grew accustomed to the gloom in the nave, and he took a pew near the back, excusing himself as he bumped through the priests and altar boys gathering for the procession up the center aisle to the brightly lit altar.

As they began intoning the penitential litanies, they paraded forward holding banners and gold crosses high under the deep blue starry heavens that adorned the high arched ceilings, the chief priest's swinging censor spreading a bluish cloud of spicy Frankincense.

It gave Rob a jolt. Incense brings the deity nigh. Carmen slipped in beside him and knelt quickly to pray, crossing herself. She continued to look straight ahead as Rob angrily confronted her in a low voice, "What are you doing with these drug dealers?" he choked, "I can't believe what is going down."

"It's worse than you know. I wish I could never speak to them again," she whispered throatily, "because of what they must've done to Kevin. They claim it was not them, that it was some of Noriega's goons, and that Noriega forced them into this business after their arrest and trial. Who knows? You have to help me Rob. I tried to refuse to be a part of it; that's why I moved to Ottawa."

"Why didn't you contact me when you first arrived?" he hissed.

"Rob, my brothers didn't know where I was when I first arrived. Unfortunately, the friends I was staying with ran into Ines Cecelia Barbosa at a Latin dance club. She's called the Godmother. She's from Colombia. As I learned sometime later, she has links with the Medellin cartel."

"Oh my God," stammered Rob.

"At first, she was very friendly with me. I thought it was just an older woman showing me the ropes in a new place. I had no idea what she was up to. But she's turned very nasty since I moved to Ottawa. Maybe she thinks I know more than I do about what is going on. She sent Emanuel to pick me up last night, and is now insisting that he take me to a meeting tonight. I don't really know who with. Rob, I'm scared." Carmen's eyes were pleading.

Surrounding parishioners were casting disapproving sideways glances, shushing them.

Ignoring them, Rob whispered, "For God's sake, it could be extremely dangerous for you. She is trying to tie you in so you will be silent. Can't you just jump into my car and we'll go back to Ottawa??

"You don't understand. I have to go with them, or they'll come to get me in Ottawa. My life will be unlivable."

"So... where are they picking you up?"

"Emanuel's picking me up at Marie-Sol's where I'm staying. Then we're going to the Limelight disco on Stanley Street. Please come after nine o'clock. It'll be busy and Emanuel won't be expecting anything, so likely won't recognize you if you keep your distance. Watch for me to go to the ladies room and meet me on the way."

They left separately without acknowledging each other. Rob lost no time finding a telephone booth and calling the drug squad contacts Ted Czernak had set up for him.

The bouncer at the Limelight didn't much like the looks of Rob and his two buddies, Mario Tremblay and Serge Mainville. But when they flashed their drug-squad IDs, he bowed with a sneer and with a sweep of his arm, waived them in despite the jeans, black turtle-neck sweaters, and leather bomber jackets with bulges. Dark brown shit-kickers with heavy composite soles completed their dance ensembles, totally out of step with the gaudy sequined lycra body suits with bell-bottoms flashing in the light and the daring mini-skirts and tight halter tops shouting come on and get me!

Masses of writhing people ignited momentarily in searchlights and flashing disco balls. The pulsing James Brown beat from the disc-jockey momentarily wiped out all other thought. They staggered and elbowed through the dancers to the bar, where Serge and Mario ordered beers and Rob a martini on the rocks.

As Rob's eyes searched the room for Carmen and Emanuel, waves of scantily clad disco babes, cross-dressers in white feathers and leathers, and hundreds of wannabes writhed and pounded in music and lights. The disco music felt good – it was music that delivered on the promises of the revolution of the 1960s. Make love, not war.

Rob tipped his drink and looked over the scene. The Montréal of the late seventies was really a city of broken dreams that had its roots in Quebec's Quiet Revolution of the sixties, and the cosmopolitan explosion that was Expo '67, Terre des hommes. Pavilions from countries around the world still graced the skyline on Isle St. Helene. He smiled. Was this the recovery?

Touching his head, he remembered the 1969 inaugural season of the Montréal Expos, when baseball fever gripped the city. After that came the downers. The Front de Liberation de Quebec that kidnapped and murdered politicians, and then the October crisis, followed by the War Measures Act and martial law. Tight.

He looked down and swirled his drink. The billion-dollar boondoggle Olympics that Mayor Jean Drapeau claimed couldn't have a deficit any more than a man could have a baby left future generations with enormous debt. Strange things happen.

This was followed by the sobering election of the separatist Parti Québecois in 1976, which shattered yet more dreams and fueled an Anglophone exodus, igniting other dreams of Québec nationalists. Yes, Quebec had come of age.

Someone jostled his drink pressing past him to the bar. He looked at her sideways. Expo baseball cap and the tightest t-shirt and shortest mini he had ever seen. She smelled good. Patchouli. Warm. She smiled. Hot. She ordered a drink.

Rob pitched back what was left of his martini and asked for another. So disco music had become the new salvation for Montrealers, and discotheques their new cathedrals. He smiled and looked around, feeling more charitable now. French and English, Italians and Latinos managed their tiffs and were expending their energies and frustrations outdoing each other in fantastic dancing and outrageous outfits, flashing in the lights. Sweating, clasping, burning.

"Becha there are more coke dealers here than pimps!" shouted Mario in Rob's ear, grinning and taking a pull on his beer. It brought him back to their unpleasant job. Serge was somewhat less obtrusive as he eased his sunglasses out of an inside pocket and surveyed the scene.

Just as KC and the Sunshine Band's first number was coming to a close, Rob spotted Carmen rising from a sidewall banquette half way up the dance floor. He watched for a moment as she seemed likely to be heading for the ladies room and glanced in their direction.

"Call of nature," Rob grinned to Mario, and plunking his

glass on the bar, turned and headed for the washrooms. He glanced back to be sure that Emanuel was not following her, but he seemed to be in deep conversation with the two men from Le Jardin.

Rob moved swiftly and caught up with her, grabbing her arm in the dark hallway leading to the ladies room, where several couples were taking respite, grateful to be out of the thunderous dance music, and embracing passionately in the gloom.

Carmen turned abruptly, pushed him hard against the wall and kissed him.

"Wish this could be real for the rest of our lives," she caught her breath. Then, holding his lapels, she spoke quietly into his chest.

"There's something big going down. They plan to meet on the waterfront in Old Montreal, the Alexandra Pier I think. I said I don't want to go, but Ines is here... I'm so scared." Carmen pulled him closer and cuddled protectively into Rob.

Suddenly, over her shoulder, Rob made out the figure of Emanuel silhouetted in flashing lights at the end of the corridor, moving towards them.

"Quick," he said, and pushed Carmen towards the ladies' room door, "Emanuel is coming." He turned to face into a corner behind a couple kissing feverishly and leaned against the wall, arm above his head, as if about to be sick.

A few minutes after Carmen and the group left the Limelight, Rob was piling into the back seat of an unmarked squad car, with Mario at the wheel. In the other front seat, Serge was calling on the radio, "Double backup required, bottom of Jacques Cartier, destination Alexandra Pier."

Mario did his best to keep pace with Emanuel's Audi, at a distance, but he lost it by the time they arrived near the pier. Two other unmarked cars had materialised behind them. They drove into an old multi-story car park on the quay, to find rows and rows of parked cars, belonging to night-time revellers in Old Montreal no doubt, but no apparent drug dealers in sight. Mario and Serge got out to confer with the others.

Serge suddenly stopped dead, "Are those car lights shining across the water from behind that old Customs shed on Bickerdike Wharf?" he said in French. The wharf loomed thirty feet above the black water of the St. Laurent below, about two hundred yards from where they stood. The other nodded. In moments, the squad cars were quietly on their way around to the wharf, lights out. They came to a halt behind the customs shed. A door stood open at the end of the abandoned customs building, stairs leading into darkness on the second floor.

"Wait! I'll go up to see what's going on," Serge whispered hoarsely. "Be right back!"

Snow muffled most of the sounds of feet. The squad car doors stood open, engines off, a few yards down the access road. In a few moments, Serge reappeared from the stairs.

"There are four cars on the pier," he said breathlessly, "parked two and two, pointed this way. One big Suburban looks like the bikers, and the other two are the Latinos and the women from the disco. Let's drive two of the squad cars around the corner and block their exit. You other guys, follow behind the cars to maintain cover. We'll try to arrest them all. Jean-Paul and Jacques, go upstairs and cover us from the open windows up there. Shout after we start to let them know you are there."

"I suppose there's not much use in saying this," Rob cautioned, "but a young woman is here under duress and has nothing to do with the drug dealers' operations, except that she's related. She's the one that told us about the meet. So we have to protect her. The short older woman is probably Inez, the Godmother from the Medellin cartel. Could be dangerous."

There were nods and murmurs from the others, and the raising of eyebrows. "Just how do you know this, Rob?" demanded Mario.

"She's an acquaintance of mine from a consular case a long time ago in Panama, and is now a friend in Ottawa. She's been my source of information and is really why I'm here tonight – to try and keep her out of trouble. But it looks like that's going to be difficult."

"Okay, we'll try, but they're not a very friendly bunch. You stay here behind the customs shed."

With Jean-Paul and Jacques heading up the stairs, two of the squad cars began to ease around the corner. Serge and Mario, crept low behind, guns in hand. The group was gathered in front of the cars looking at documents in the headlights.

"Alt! Police!" shouted Mario, "Les mains en haut!"

At this, the group froze, then two bikers grabbed guns from under their jackets and headed for the Suburban. Rob came around from behind the building and into the glare of the headlights, looking for Carmen. At the same instant, the passenger door of Emanuel's Audi flung open, and Carmen dashed into the light and towards Rob. As Carmen ran between Rob and the bikers, two shots rang out- then a volley of shots from the upstairs window silenced both bikers- as she staggered, and fell into Rob's arms.

Blood seeped rapidly through Carmen's white parka, as Rob screamed, "Call an ambulance!" Pain was spreading through his own chest as he sank to his knees, holding her.

He could already hear the sirens when she turned her ashen face up to him and pleaded, "Rob... take me away from here... I love you... I'm sorry."

CHAPTER 19

Morning light streamed through a tall window of the old gray-stone building. Rob struggled to raise his arm under a tight sheet. It seemed not to be connected to him. He gave up. He managed to blink open his eyes. Hanging above his head, only a silhouette against the light, was a plastic intravenous bag. Into his consciousness seeped pinging sounds and blinking lights. An array of blood pressure and heart beat monitoring equipment surrounded Rob, thumping and blinking lights that seemed to be connected to him through tubes and wires. At least he could hear what seemed to be a steady, slow heartbeat.

He felt no pain, only a dreamy wakefulness as if he was floating, and managed to look down past his chin under the flimsy hospital gown. There seemed to be a massive dressing on his chest.

A movement to his right. He looked up as Serge pushed past the surgeon standing at the foot of his bed.

"Welcome to the Royal Victoria Hospital!" he grinned. "Your girlfriend was not so lucky. She took two bullets for you. I guess there was some damage to the kidney and an enormous loss of blood. Lucky to be here, but she's not out of the woods. One bullet came right through her and hit you, apparently lodged in your rib. It slowed down though, so not much damage."

"But she's alive?" gasped Rob, alarmed, shooting pain in his chest now with the struggle to prop himself up on his elbows. "Can I see her?"

"You had better lie back," commanded a doctor who seemed to appear out of nowhere, pushing Rob's shoulder back onto the pillow. "You won't be going anywhere for a day or two. We've taken the bullet out of you. She is alive, but barely. She needs a lot more work."

"Neither will she be going anywhere any time soon," said Serge, "She's under arrest."

"But Serge, you can't mean that," struggled Rob. "After all she's been through... you know none of us would be here without her tip-off."

"I know where your heart is, Rob. But do you really know what she was involved in? The circumstantial evidence does not look good. After all, she was in a car on the wrong side of a drug bust.

"By the way, those were shipping documents the bikers were looking at when we surprised them. They led my colleagues straight to a consignment from St. Vincent in the port train yards. Very imaginative. Cases of tins marked 'hearts of palm' filled with high-grade cocaine. Not a bad effort. Dogs wouldn't have caught it. Street value many millions."

"Wow," wheezed Rob through gritted teeth.

"Most puzzling of all they came into Canada on two diplomatic passports, one in your name and the other a Claude Sarasin. Know anything about it?"

Rob was up on his elbows again, "They were stolen from us in Costa Rica. Claude was the consular clerk at the Embassy."

"The photos were changed of course and I assume some other details."

"Do you have some next of kin, your wife or someone you would like to notify of your condition?" cut in the surgeon anxiously waving Serge away with his clip board. Obviously too much conversation for Rob's condition.

"We couldn't call anyone when you were brought in through emergency, because you weren't conscious. There's a phone on the bedside table, and I'll get someone to help, if you like."

Sophie was shocked. "Why haven't you called?" was the demand.

She was incredulous with Rob's explanation of why he was in Montréal and how on earth he came to get shot. She was more than dubious about his involvement in the whole affair.

She remembered well the terrifying saga of Carmen Torres and the Panama murder, and how they had been forced to leave San Jose before their posting had been completed. She was angry. But, at the same time, she desperately wanted to see Rob and be with him. She insisted on flying to Montréal on the earliest plane she could catch, to Rob's dismay.

Some days later Rob was able to confront Carmen in her hospital bed. She was pale and very weak, still in intensive care, with monitors connected.

"Carmen," Rob whispered hoarsely, "are you okay?"

Her eyes fluttered open, then the deep brown pools brightened and she fixed on Rob's.

"Oh God, Rob – we're alive," she struggled to get up. He

pushed her down gently. "I was so worried. Are you going to be okay?"

"Sure, thanks to you. But the doctors say you need more surgery before they let you out. So I wanted to come by before I go back to work in Ottawa."

"You mean you're leaving me?" She clutched his arm.

"Well I can't do much here, so I'll be back in a few days to see how you're progressing."

"What's going to happen to me, Rob?"

"I thought you could tell me. The drug squad has many open questions and so do I."

"Questions?" Her pale face reflected panic.

"Serge from the drug squad, said Pedro and Hernando came in on two diplomatic passports, mine and Claude Sarasin's."

She was straining, "What? The last time I saw your passport was in Bocas del Toro. I have no clue what happened to them."

"No? Well how did they come to be with your brothers, and used for the drug smuggling?"

"That's unfair Rob."

"That's all the time you can have, Mr. Kingman. You'll have to leave now." The specialist nurse, face stern, motioned him to the door.

Rob took one last shot, "What about Kevin Voth? Did your brothers kill him?"

Carmen turned into the pillow. Tears streamed down her face.

CHAPTER 20

"Well, well, it's the hero of the drug wars. Congratulations on busting up the gang. How's the war wound?" Colonel Gregory grinned as he looked up from his morning paper. He was sitting with his coffee in the guest chair in Rob's office again. First morning back.

Rob sidled gently into the chair behind his desk, grimacing with the twinges of pain in his chest as he sat. "It's good to be here after all that. What a surprise I must say! When I started down the road to Montréal a week ago Saturday, I had no idea what I might be in for."

"It was certainly a surprise to me when I found out. I had no clue about any of your involvement either, but Ted Czernak filled me in pretty well when you didn't turn up last week. So I've been minding the shop and keeping things ticking over. Thought you might like a briefing on what's happening."

"Yes, that would be great. A friend of mine from Panama City took a couple of bullets for me, so she's in much worse shape. Expect she'll be out of the hospital in a week or ten days."

"You know, Rob, I always knew there was something of the Galahad in you," Gregory smiled, "but we'll leave that for another time. Matters are pressing."

"Cosmos 954, you'll be pleased to know, is still in a decaying orbit – it's now tumbling and will come down any day. So you haven't missed the fun. The orbit's track is over Pine Point, so no doubt the Soviets were spying on the uranium mine on the north shore of Lake Athabaska and the northern early warning lines."

"I am pleased to know," offered Rob.

"On another front and perhaps right up your alley for your apparent interest in salacious involvements," the colonel said, bobbing his head, "three of the five Cubans who are training in CIDA courtesy of the PM's new coop-eration and development agreement with Fidel are getting into it fully, shagging some of our program officers. Haven't lost the Latino touch. Hard to maintain objectivity and security you might say?"

"Why don't we just send them home?" Rob queried.

"One might think that could be the thing to do, but the PM won't let us take action. He doesn't want to disrupt political progress with the Cubans; I guess he's into embracing them," he grinned. "After all, the government has no business in the bedrooms of consenting adults, isn't that what he says?"

"And another one for you, wait for it... we have a CBC producer selling photocopies of biographies from the Parliamentary Guide to KGB agents for five hundred dollars a crack. He thinks it's a joke and gets him some pin money because they could just buy the book. But wait till the Soviets up the ante and blackmail him for taking money from them when they want to know more about MPs' compromising activities. Might be an idea for you to call him in and privately brief him on the dangers of this activity, before we have to whack him with the Official Secrets Act down the road. All in all, a rather entertaining agenda, wouldn't you say?"

A couple of days later, Rob was sitting at a private table in the Suisha Gardens, waiting for an overweight, chain smoking, Marty Prendergast to show up, when the hostess brought an attractive dark-haired woman to him instead. She held out her hand to be shaken.

"Mr. Kingman? I'm Kristin Andersen. Marty sends his apologies. He's been unavoidably detained at the last minute, so he sent me along to meet with you. Said you would probably much rather have lunch with me than him anyways."

She bobbed her pert head, and slid her CBC reporter's bag off her shoulder and onto the floor beside the chair.

"There must be some mistake," stumbled Rob as he sat down. He couldn't take his eyes off her. "What I had intended to discuss with Mr. Prendergast is highly confidential and very personal."

"Well... Marty and I are more than workmates. We're more, how shall I put it, soul mates? So personal is okay," she smiled.

"Even so, I'm not sure this is the kind of thing that I can discuss with you, from a security point of view."

"You mean it's not about that spy satellite Cosmos 954 coming down in the middle of Montréal, as your tantalizing press release warned? Ahh, I know. Marty and I were at the Soviet national day reception a few weeks ago when a couple of weird guys, undoubtedly KGB, cornered him and asked him for some information on Members of Parliament. Is that what it is?"

"Well as a matter of fact, it is. How's that going?"

"Well, actually. It's something of a joke around the office. Marty has gotten five hundred bucks for a couple of pages photocopied out of the Parliamentary Guide. You're not going to say that that's a serious problem are you? Suckering these wise guys for beer money? He's been very open about it, taking us out for drinks. Uh, how do you know about this in your exalted position in intelligence for the Cabinet Office? Is he under surveillance?"

"He's not, but you know our counterintelligence people intercept some of the communications of known intelligence operatives under court order."

"You mean Marty's collateral damage? Well isn't that dirty pool! Who would have thunk?" she mused, and tossed back a shot of sake.

"Yes, who would have? Ever since former KGB officer Igor Gouzenko came in from the cold and spilled the beans on Soviet spying methods, some members of the embassy have been under surveillance. The embassy tried to discredit him as a mere cipher clerk, but he seems to have been a lot more than a technician.

"Anyway, Marty also needs to know that what he is doing is a typical lead into entrapment by the KGB. This is the message you need to take back to him. They will start to ramp up by asking for more detailed gossip about the MPs, like who they are seeing on the side, or how their expense claims are going, or whether their travel is justified. Bigger money is offered. You know what I mean? Water cooler chat: easy but compromising tidbits that could be radio news stories, but also could be used as leverage.

"And it's the same with Marty. Once he has taken their

money, they will hint that it would not be easy to explain why he did so if it should come to light through an anonymous call to his employers. And it just gets more complicated. Better to avoid the problem than to have to deal with an uncomfortable and politically compromising situation down the road. No?"

"Yes. I'll pass it along. Though I'm not sure he'll heed the warning. This is excellent sushi," Kristin said slowly, saucily, her lips forming a perfect "O" around a piece of tuna as it disappeared into her mouth. She toasted him with another small cup of sake. Rob was surprised. Or was she mocking?

After their goodbyes, the buzz in his head continued, as Rob indulged in more extravagant visions of his surprising lunch companion on his walk back along Sparks Street Mall to his office. These meanderings were quickly swept away on Rob's return by Ted Czernak,.

"Looks like your very good friends Pedro and Hernan are on the move since their release."

"Release? Surely not. Has Carmen Torres been released from custody as well?"

"Nope, apparently not. Serge's note through channels doesn't say much about her, except that there was not enough direct evidence to hold the two Latinos. Evidently, her association with the 'godmother' must be an issue. Prosecutions are going ahead against the surviving biker-for attempted murder, in addition to the drug trafficking charges."

"Where are they headed? Does the message say?"

"You mean Pedro and Hernan? Yes, somewhere in the

Caribbean. An island called Bequia. Ever heard of it?"

Rob was now more determined than ever to confront them.

CHAPTER 21

The ancient seagoing car ferry plunged on through the surprisingly deep swells in the mid-Caribbean. Rob braced himself against the pipe rail in the bow, enjoying the warm salt spray that hit his face from time to time and turned his blonde hair dark. For hours, his mind had raced over the many coincidences that had brought him to this two hour passage between Kingstown on St. Vincent's, and Port Elizabeth on Bequia, the second largest island in the Grenadines. He felt a wrench in his gut over his hidden mission, especially over keeping it from his unsuspecting family.

Sophie and young Julia were entertaining each other on the stern sun-deck, Sophie laughing as the youngster tried to maintain her balance. She was so beautiful with her golden curls and blue eyes. The three-year old squealed delightedly as she made experimental dashes between Marilyn and Roger. Sophie's cousin and her husband were CBC types who took time from their travels to make a winter pilgrimage to this part of the world every year for beach time and skin diving. They had been the perfect carrot for Sophie. The timing was fortuitous.

Rob hadn't really wanted to expose any of his family to the kind of dangers he anticipated, but he had become convinced that following Pedro and Hernan to the island would yield the key to getting Carmen released. His discussions with her had lead him to this conclusion. Her wounds had been serious enough to require surgical repairs to some organs. She was very keen for his occasional visits that lasted until she was remanded to custody a few weeks later.

"You know, Rob," she'd said, "I think my brothers have been busted a few times, but it never seems to stick. They always keep me out of the actual business during their visits, so I don't really know what is going on. They try to keep me out of trouble, too. Obviously it went wrong this time. I wasn't supposed to be there. Except for Ines' insistence."

It was not in his mandate to head off across the Caribbean to gather evidence on the doings of two drug dealers, but any other evidence that would release Carmen had not been easy to come by. And Serge had not been willing to share much about why Pedro and Hernan had been released without charges. He said pointedly the drug squad would not be following up in Bequia.

So, as they rounded the island headland and sailed the final stretch to Port Elizabeth, he began to contemplate how he might keep his family apart from his very personal mission.

Now that they were in calmer waters, he lifted his hand to his face and wiped off some of the salt spray. Dave McCracken, the deputy secretary to Cabinet, would not have been keen to let him go had he known the true nature of Rob's intentions. Understanding this, Rob had not mentioned anything of them when he had asked for time in the sun for R and R after his Montréal ordeal. He was on his own. Solo.

Bequia was an underdeveloped backwater where the odd tourist went to commune with Rastas on the beach, with their longboats ready to fish, and Jamaican ganja in the air. Further up-island there was a nineteenth century local whaling station, operated now by some of the original settler families. Now a small airport had been built on the east side of the island. Improving access for whom, he wondered? There were also some luxury yachts anchored in Port Elizabeth. And indeed, there was also an exclusive resort without a name on the beach south of Port Elizabeth.

Rob touched his head... recalling rumors in Costa Rica before they left about the fugitive investor Robert Vesco buying up properties in the Caribbean a few years before, and wondered to himself whether he had expanded into the drug trade. That it was here was a long shot.

Sophie's cousins Marilyn and Roger were proving to be excellent hosts on the island which they knew well from their annual winter pilgrimages. And they gladly shared a rented villa near Princess Margaret Beach, also south of Port Elizabeth along the shore.

Rob and Sophie plunged into glorious days of snorkelling on the beautiful coral reefs that ringed the island. The myriads of tropical fish, colored, striped, and inquisitive, bumped their masks. Others skittered away swiftly. Roger and Marilyn took to gathering seashells with Julia on the beach and playing in the surf. There were tourist trips with Noel in his gaudily painted truck to the top of Mount Pleasant, the highest point on the island, from where you could see the whaling station at Petit Nevis that his family was still involved with, and the defunct sugar plantation further down.

Rob had almost forgotten the mission that lurked in the recesses of his mind when he spotted Pedro and Hernan earlier in the day at the dive shack on the beach, just south of the Frangipani Hotel, where they sat having a cool drink at outdoor tables. At the time, Roger had pointed out a gazebo like structure and said it was the diving center for many islanders. Skin diving excursions to favorite spots were arranged there, as were lessons. Roger had proposed Rob come with him on his next diving outing, as he was quite experienced. Sometime later, they had all gone south along the beach past the dive-shack and eventually made their way home to the villa.

They went up that evening to Fernando's Hideaway, a funky local restaurant perched high up a hillside in the rain forest. They ducked through massive tropical foliage that shrouded the entrance. Fernando's sister Cecilia smiled a greeting, chirping gaily as she showed them to a rustic handmade wooden table near the edge of the wide veranda, perched on poles in the green canopy. As chairs scraped gently and they sat down, smiling, the evening sea breeze wafted over them soft and fresh. It soothed away the burning heat of the sand and sea that still lingered on their skins.

As Cecelia was offering them the best on the menu, sea bass caught by Fernando's own hand that morning, a larger party of six created a commotion at the entrance. They were shown to another table off in a corner somewhat down the veranda from them.

"Sophie, why don't you switch sides with me so you can

see the view out the front?" Rob demanded with alarm, so that he could have his back toward the new arrivals, Pedro, Hernan and their companion, Captain Carlos Rios. With his back towards them, they would be less likely to recognize him. He was stunned to see Rios, who until that moment had faded from his memory.

The three men engaged in animated conversation, heads down, with the three beautiful women accompanying them, pausing only to order brusquely. They hadn't noticed him, not suspecting in the least he might be there. Still, Rob was tense and stressed throughout the meal. He hardly tasted the fish smothered in a delicious mango salsa. His bananas, rice and beans were untouched.

"You're not talking much, Rob. In fact, you're looking kind of gray. Are you feeling sick? Maybe a little too much sun?" Roger asked with concern. "I really had hoped you would like the food. It's my favorite on the island."

"No, no, it's wonderful," Rob protested, "but I really am feeling rather off. Do you mind if we head back to the villa and turn in early?" He was greeted with a chorus of groans.

He tossed and turned fitfully under the mosquito netting. Even though a cool breeze wafted off the Caribbean through an open window, he sweated profusely. By about two o'clock, he had formulated a plan. He leaned lovingly over Sophie's slumbering figure, "I'm going for a walk," he whispered hoarsely, so as not to wake the others. "It's a beautiful night, but I can't sleep." He kissed her firmly on the lips. She responded and sat up on one elbow. "Take care," she smiled and kicked off the damp sheet, her beautiful nakedness open in the dim light. Then, she sank back into sun-exhausted sleep.

On the road outside the villa, he looked back, reluctant to leave. But he moved forward, casting a shadow under a bright, nearly full moon as he strode along the road down to the beach. Reaching the brow of the hill, he could hear gentle surf on the rocky beach below. The dark sea stretched out before him in the bay.

When he turned right and left the road, he struggled a bit and slipped once, falling quite heavily on an elbow. The rocky and root strewn path led down the hill and north along the coast through a small forested area past a waterfall. The scent of Jasmine and Moon Flower filled the air. A chorus of cicadas fell quiet as he passed.

He brushed a bug off his ear. From the beach walkway, he had seen the main pink villa of an imposing private resort nestled in the palms and lush tropical garden. So his plan now was to see if Pedro and Hernan were there. He recalled that several smaller cabanas were scattered over the property and a large roofed bar with a barbecue pit and a dance floor with local murals, was to one side of the main building.

The whole property facing the sea was protected with an imposing stone wall. Armed guards had been standing at the main gate, which was flanked by huge ship anchors embedded in concrete. A wooden boardwalk ran from the main gate to a substantial jetty into the blue Caribbean. Two powerful motor launches were docked alongside and a couple of luxurious yachts anchored offshore. Rob recalled that the guards had rudely told them to move on when they inquired whether they might sightsee on the property.

As Rob struggled to find his footing on the rocky path

down the cliff overlooking the resort, he glanced up to just make out a high chain-link fence that stretched from the wrought iron fence along the sea walk, into the darkness towards the rear through impassable tropical foliage. Now he walked cautiously along the stone wall that fronted the resort, almost at the main gates. When he reached the wrought iron gates they were tightly secured with a chain and a lock on the inside.

There were no guards in sight. Suddenly bright motion detector floodlights bathed him in near sunshine levels of light. Blinking, he turned and ducked low back along the wall the way he had come, stumbling, temporarily blinded. He reached the edge of the property and turned inland around the end of the wall, heart pounding. No one seemed to be following. Struggling his way along the chain-link fence through the dense greenery towards the rear of the complex, he tried to avoid the sharp thorns on the tips of the leaves of the sisal plants. He glanced up anxiously at the strands of barbed wire that topped it.

After thirty more yards of heavy going, he came upon a small stream, gurgling through the forest in the dark. There was a join in the fence above the small stream that had spread apart lower down. The banks had been gouged out by the water flow. He had to crouch on his knees in the water, but the fence gave way sufficiently for him to slip through.

Finally on the inside, he stood up slowly on the bank, looking intently for any sign he had been spotted. Rob took stock of his wet and disheveled clothes, stooping to brush mud and slime off his pants. He pulled out a handkerchief to pat at the blood welling on his arm from a deep scratch.

It stung. Crouching again, Rob looked around through the low foliage for any signs of guards or dogs. He could hear nothing except the resuming cicada chorus above the gurgling of the stream.

He was somewhere behind most of the cabinas, whose outlines he could see against the sky as he looked seaward. He had no idea of how he would find Pedro or Hernan in order to confront them about their sister's plight. If they were here at all.

Moving up the green shrouded path he started suddenly as he came face-to-face with a statue, a poor copy of Botticelli's Birth of Venus, smiling vaguely at him, her fountain trickling feebly in the half shell. Before he could turn to face the slight rustling behind him, he felt the hard barrel of a gun against the back of his head. Rios said quietly, "What a strange place to meet again, Señor Kingman."

Then blackness.

CHAPTER 21

Rob's consciousness returned to the throaty growl of powerful engines, and to the accompanying throb of a sickening headache. His eyes opened to a sideways view across the rear of the main deck of a seagoing fishing cruiser. Pedro was at the helm. Rob lay on the back bench, arms painfully trussed behind his back, wrists secured with duct tape. The back of his head hurt where he had lifted it to see what was going on. His hair had torn away from around the wound to his scalp he'd received from the pistol whipping. It stuck to the bench where his blood had dried around it.

He could make out Hernan and Captain Rios conferring urgently on a side bench, bathed in the growing strength of the dawn light. Pedro throttled back to idle as the rocks of Moon Hole tunnel came into view. Roger had told him that some of the best reef diving in the Caribbean took place off this point, a few miles southwest from Port Elisabeth.

"Wake up!" Rios commanded, having clearly lost none of his clean-cut military bearing. He scooped Rob up roughly from the bench with a swift and painful pull.

"You're going to suit up for a dive," He said. As he tore off the tape binding Rob's wrists, he demanded, "Strip down to your underwear." Rob struggled to find his balance and staggered amid-ships, rubbing his wrists.

Rios extracted a wetsuit from the bench locker Rob had lain on, along with a tank, mask and fins, and dropped them on the deck at Rob's feet. He also took out a heavy, lead-weighted diving belt for deep descent. Reluctantly Rob began putting on the gear.

"Can we talk about this?" Rob asked, "I've never been diving before."

"It doesn't matter. We're not planning on you being successful."

"But why?" asked Rob, "I only came down here to ask Pedro and Hernando about helping their sister."

"Oh, that bitch," Rios screamed into Rob's face, "Unfinished business from Panama, as far as I'm concerned. Why does she need their help?"

At that moment, Pedro hit both throttles wide open and the boat surged forward violently, prow rising as the two enormous outboards dug deep. Standing with the weights around his waist and ungainly fins on his feet, Rob fell heavily against Rios and then to his knees.

Caught off guard, Rios stepped backwards, arms flailing and then fell, the small of his back hitting the rear gunwale. From there, he tumbled into the churning wake of deep water. Stony-faced, Pedro stared straight ahead with the boat accelerating till it lifted onto the step and planed away from the island at high speed.

After a few minutes, he cut the throttles and called back, grinning, "Nice to meet you face to face. Shall we have some breakfast?"

Rob, still on his knees, was stunned. He looked rearward, but could see nothing on the calming blue sea.

"Can Rios swim? We're a long way from shore."

"Hope not. Tragic accident... I guess we should have noticed he was overboard sooner," replied Hernan, who was helping Rob get out of the wetsuit and gear.

"We've been waiting for a long time to unload him. The time was right. Came up here because he was starting to figure out that maybe the Drug Enforcement Agency was too successful in busting up our deliveries."

Shortly, Rob was dressed again in his disheveled clothes. Hernan smiled, "You look good. Let's go down to the galley and see what Pedro is rustling up for breakfast. We can probably find you a plaster for your scalp, too."

He took the cup. The smell of coffee, and then the taste, was like ambrosia to Rob. He felt as if he was back from death. Settling down at the galley table to tuck into his bacon, eggs, and beans, he was still shaking.

Pedro turned, "You must've thought we were real assholes when we didn't turn up for Carmen those years ago back in Panama."

"Yes. I couldn't figure out why you didn't re-appear. Thought you were fleeing the charges."

"Rios had taken us and Kevin to holding cells in the Palace of Justice. We didn't know why we had been arrested. Maybe our lack of legal refugee status. We only wanted to talk to Kevin about the interests of our sister. Hurry him along or get him to drop her. She was a big girl by then and could take care of herself, mostly."

"You mean you weren't UN status refugees?"

"No, no we weren't. Not like the refugees from Chile, anyway. We came across the border from Colombia. Our parents had been taken away when the FARC occupied our family *finca*. We fled to Medellin. A priest in Cartagena helped us cross the Panamanian border. We had to maintain the Chilean fiction when we got to Panama City for a time, so we wouldn't be sent back. But we never got official refugee status."

"So what happened to Kevin?"

"Rios wanted us to sign up for one of Noriega's new businesses. Had us over a barrel because of our status. We had to agree to some sort of confidentiality letter. Kevin refused outright to let us sign up and Rios had him taken away. We never saw him again. Evidently, you found his body in the Zone."

Hernan joined in, "It was quite a ride in the early days, Noriega threatening that the murder of Kevin would be pinned on us, and we could be turned out for an easy conviction. We bided our time, working in the business, waiting for the moment when we could get away. But it never came. We eventually managed to make clandestine contact with the Americans in San Jose to try and get away, after we knew Carmen had made it to Canada. But instead, they insisted we stay on and tip them off about shipments when we could."

"So that's why you were released so quickly in Montreal," Rob interrupted. "Carmen is in serious trouble. She's being held on drug trafficking charges, resisting arrest, and assault. You name it. Can you help?"

"We tried at the time in Montréal, but we were only able to deal with police and administration of justice people who were not in the know about our status. That official word from the US government has to come through the consulate. We'll do that again for her. It should get her released."

Then Pedro added, "And we'll have to pull the plug on our drug operations and get our US asylum now. It's all over. Trying to explain Rios' 'accident' to Noriega would end it all for us."

"You know, I owe my life to Carmen. She took two bullets for me, and I owe her, even though I never would have been there without her."

"She loved you Rob. You worked a miracle getting her out of Noriega's clutches in Panama. So sorry it cost you friends. Let's drink to success, and we'll get you back to your villa for brunch with your wife!"

They raised their coffee cups that now held a shot of rum. Hernan grinned at Rob over his, "Better make up a good story, 'cause you look like you've had a very hard night!"

CPSIA information can be obtained
at www.ICGtesting.com
Printed in the USA
LVOW11s0747060418
572543LV00001B/135/P